KNIGHT BEFORE CHRISTMAS

A Lauderdale Knights Garland Grove Holiday Novel

KAT MIZERA

Edits: Taylor Bellitto

Cover Design: Dar Albert, Wicked Smart Designs

✿ Created with Vellum

CHAPTER ONE

Remy

I leaned back against the plush leather seats and loosened my tie as the limo inched through the snow of an unexpected New York City storm.

"I don't know if we're going to make your flight, sir," the driver called back to me.

"Do your best," I told him. Weather wasn't something anyone could control so there was no need to express frustration, especially to my driver.

I sent a text to my assistant, Fiona, and asked her to call the airline's customer service number to see if there were any backup flights available if I missed this one. I was flying to Vancouver, British Columbia and from there, renting a car and driving to Garland Grove. I didn't have time for this trip, but going forward I'd have even less, so it was now or never. Besides, my mother was in Vancouver, so I'd be able to spend a few days with her during the holidays.

Picking up my phone again, I called the older of my two younger brothers, Kingston.

"Hey." He sounded half asleep, which was no surprise since he was a rock star who was currently on tour.

"Did I wake you?" I asked.

"Yeah, but it's cool. What's up?"

"Needed to run something past you."

"Shoot."

"In Dad's infinite wisdom, he left us an ice arena."

"He left us an ice...arena?" Kingston sounded as confused as I'd been. "The lawyer didn't say anything about that when he read the will."

"It was part of the everything-not-mentioned-above stuff. The lawyer sent me a box of papers and deeds and shit, so I forwarded it all to my attorney and asked him to sort through it. It's deeded to the three of us. You, me and Ashton." Ashton was our youngest brother, who was only twenty and in college.

"You're not going to keep it, are you?" he asked.

"I don't think so, but I'm on my way to visit now. You'll never guess where it's located."

"Garland Grove?" he asked, chuckling.

"Yup."

"He didn't have a romantic or sentimental bone in his body for anything except that place. You think we have a whole family of half-siblings living there?"

I groaned. "Jesus, don't even put that out in the universe, man."

He laughed. "Look, if you want to buy me out, I'm cool with it. I have zero interest in an ice rink in Bumfuck, British Columbia."

"I'm thinking Ashton will be excited to get a check from me," I mused. "Since I was definitely not his favorite person after the reading of the will."

"Well, Dad put his entire inheritance in a trust with you as the administrator. What twenty-year-old would be happy about that?"

We both laughed. "You're lucky he didn't do the same with yours."

He snorted. "Fuck him and his inheritance. I'll donate it to charity. I don't need his fucking money." Kingston and our father had not been close. *At all.*

"I don't either," I replied, "but I feel like I should check out the rink, see what's what, before I sell it off sight unseen."

"Wait, is that the place he said is magic or some such bullshit? Like everyone who skates on the outdoor rink during the holidays falls in love?"

"That's the place."

I could picture him rolling his eyes.

"Look out, bro, or you'll be married before the end of the year."

"It's November thirtieth. I highly doubt it." I was a confirmed bachelor, as was Kingston, so it was a joke between us about who would succumb to matrimony first. I was thirty-five, of course, to his twenty-seven, which meant statistically it would be me. But I was fighting it for all I was worth. Women had been nothing but a hassle as far as I was concerned.

"Friendly wager?" he asked.

I laughed. "Sure. What are we betting?"

"If you lose, you come onstage and sing with me at the venue of my choice."

I cringed since I couldn't sing for shit and Kingston's band, Onyx Knight, was one of the biggest rock bands in the world right now.

"Fine," I said, since there was no way I was getting married in thirty-one days. "But it has to be at a relatively convenient time—I did just buy an expansion hockey team. However, on the flip side of the bet, if you lose, you play hockey with me at my yearly charity event."

"Ugh." Kingston groaned. He liked hockey about as much as I enjoyed singing. "Fine. It's a bet."

"Love you, kid."

"Love you too, asshole." He disconnected.

I put my phone away as the limo got on the highway that would take us to LaGuardia.

"We might make it," the driver called over his shoulder.

"Excellent."

I didn't want to miss the flight because I'd probably change my mind completely and just head to Florida. I'd just bought a house in Fort Lauderdale on the Intracoastal Waterway. After bidding for an NHL franchise in said city two years ago, it was now official, and I'd just left a meeting with my investors. I hadn't thought a pro hockey team in South Florida would garner much interest, but my business colleagues had surprised me. Now we were less than a year from our inaugural season and I had so much damn work to do.

A trip to British Columbia was a huge inconvenience but the holidays were around the corner so it was the perfect time for a little R&R before the new year. There was also a tiny part of me that wanted to visit Garland Grove, perhaps for the last time, because it was the last place I had any good memories of my childhood. Dad had loved Garland Grove, and we would go for a few weeks at Christmas every year. It was where I'd learned to ice-skate and had fallen in love with hockey.

We'd stopped going a few years after Kingston was born and by then I was involved in hockey, baseball, and all kinds of other things so it hadn't been a big deal. Now that I was on my way back, memories suddenly flooded me, and I wondered what my father had been thinking by leaving us the rink there. A rink we hadn't even known he owned.

My phone rang as I got to the airport and Ashton's name flashed on the screen. Kingston had probably texted him with an update and I answered, saying, "Kingston tell you to call me?"

Ashton chuckled. "He texted me and said, 'Remy has a surprise for you. You should call him.' I can only imagine what you've got up your sleeve."

I told him about the rink and he was as unimpressed as Kingston had been. "Oh, yay. Another asset I don't have access to."

"Actually, I'm probably going to sell it and we can split it three ways. I don't need the money and I'm happy to give you your share once it's sold."

"You will?"

"I know you're pissed off about Dad making me the administrator of your trust fund, but that was his doing, not mine. And the way he set it up, I legally can't give you the money until you're twenty-five even if I wanted to."

"I know, but it still sucks," he muttered.

"You're twenty and have a free ride playing college hockey. Mom and I give you everything you need, including spending money. I don't know what you would do with millions of dollars at your age anyway."

"I guess."

"So, how's hockey?" Like me, Ashton had started playing hockey at a young age and was a star player at North Dakota University.

"Good. Having a decent season, though I've been in a slump the last couple of weeks."

"Get out of your head," I told him. "Just let your body do the work. It knows what to do. If you start thinking about shit, you mess with your vibe."

"You coming to any games?" he asked. "Haven't seen you since the season opener."

"I know. I'm sorry. Work is crazy. But I'll get there after the first of the year. Promise."

"Cool."

"I'll let you know what I find out about the rink and we'll go from there, okay?"

"Yup. Talk soon."

"Love you, kiddo."

"You too!" He disconnected and I chuckled to myself. They drove me crazy sometimes, but my brothers were awesome.

———

There were no brand-name hotels in Garland Grove, so I'd booked a room at a small bed and breakfast called the Christmas Mountain B&B. My room was clean and spacious, and the four-poster bed was comfortable. I propped myself against the headboard and turned on the TV as I scrolled through my email on my laptop. Normally, I wouldn't dream of going to bed this early but I had a lot going on with the new hockey team and my day would probably start at five in the morning tomorrow.

When I'd been drafted to play pro hockey at eighteen, I'd never dreamed that an unknown heart defect would force me into retirement at thirty or that I'd subsequently make hundreds of millions by starting a line of sporting goods. And if anyone had suggested I was going to buy an NHL hockey team of my own someday, I'd have laughed in their faces. Yet here I was.

My father had made it clear that his sons had to make it on their own before getting any of his money, though that hadn't really applied to me since I'd gone pro at eighteen. I'd played two seasons in the minor leagues before getting called up and after that, I hadn't needed him or his money. I'd had the option of going to college—Dad offered to pay for all of us to go—but professional hockey was far more of a temptation. Kingston had gone to Juilliard and studied music, shocking the hell out of everyone when he went from classical violin and piano to hard rock, but he was so damn talented.

Ashton was more like me, taking my advice about going to college because we'd seen firsthand how unexpectedly a professional athlete's career could end. The same heart defect that had ended my career had ended Dad's life, because he'd been too stubborn to get it looked at or have the corrective surgery. Kingston and Ashton had been tested as well, and they were okay, which had been a huge relief, but Dad had thought he was invincible.

So had I once upon a time. Then there had been the heart attack. Right on the ice, in the middle of a game. One of my teammates had started chest compressions as they yelled for a team doctor and paramedics. The story I'd been told, since I didn't remember this part at all, was that they'd used the defibrillator to shock my heart three times before it started beating again. I'd had surgery that night and I'd retired six months later.

My life was good—great, even—so I didn't like to dwell on the past but I would have been lying if I said I didn't miss hockey. That was a big part of the reason I'd been excited about buying an expansion team. Just being in an arena every day, being part of the day-to-day process of running a team, would help fill that empty part of my soul. It wouldn't be the same as actually playing, but it would help. I'd been involved with the business end of things, for a team that didn't exist yet, and I was already obsessed. I couldn't wait for the Lauderdale Knights to become a reality.

An urgent succession of knocks on the door made me jump and I got out of bed, walking over to peer through the peephole.

"Mr. Knight? It's Rudy." The owner of the bed and breakfast stood outside the door.

"Hi." I opened the door.

"Sorry to bother you, but there's a fire down at the rink and we're going down to see if anyone needs help. I just wanted you to know there wouldn't be anyone on-site in case you need something but—"

"Wait, did you say the rink? The Garland Grove Ice Arena?" I asked.

"That's the only one in town."

"The arena I just inherited from my father?" I turned and started digging around in my suitcase for my sneakers. "Wait for me—I'm coming too!"

CHAPTER TWO

Noelle

I'd just gotten out of the shower when I smelled the smoke. The smell was too strong to be coming from outside, but I couldn't imagine what might be causing smoke. I dried off quickly, yanking on sweats and a long-sleeve T-shirt before stuffing my feet in my sandals and hurrying out of the locker room.

When I got into the hallway, it was filled with smoke and I turned around, going back into the locker room to grab my duffel bag and phone. If there was a fire, there was no way I'd leave any of my meager belongings to burn. I wasn't particularly worried yet, since the arena was old and run-down. Things broke and went wrong all the time, so I tended to take things like this in stride.

The smoke was pretty thick, though.

Opting to err on the side of caution, I turned right and headed down to one of the emergency exits. Once I was outside, I could call our maintenance man, Dwayne, and have him come down to see what was going on.

I opened the door and was immediately assaulted by a combination of ice-cold wind and a barrage of lights and sounds. There were at least three fire trucks and five police cars, all with lights flashing, surrounded by dozens of people.

"Noelle!" I turned to see Dwayne hurrying toward me.

"What's going on?" I asked.

"You weren't answering your phone!" he said, breathing hard. "They wouldn't let me in to look for you."

"I was in the shower," I said weakly, looking around. "What's going on?"

"Zamboni caught on fire, which spread to a bunch of stuff in the storage rooms too. They have it under control but you scared the crap out of me, girl." He gave me a hard look and I swallowed uncomfortably.

Dwayne was my friend, my coworker, and one of the only people who sort of knew my secret.

"Is this her?" One of the policemen came running over to us.

"Yes. She was in the shower."

"I had no idea something was wrong," I said quietly. "I didn't mean to worry anyone. I spilled ketchup on myself when I was closing down the concession stand, so I thought I'd shower…"

The policeman nodded. "You're lucky it wasn't worse."

"I am. Thank you all for thinking of me."

"You look cold," Dwayne said, taking off his jacket. "Here."

"That's okay, I'll just go to my car and—"

"Parking lot's closed right now." He dropped the jacket over my shoulders. "And your damn hair is wet." He shook his head. "You can't keep this up, Noelle."

"I'm fine," I mumbled.

"Is this her?" A loud, unfamiliar voice made me jump and I turned in surprise.

I didn't know the guy, but he looked pissed, and I took an inadvertent step back.

"Noelle, this is Remington Knight, the new owner of the arena," Dwayne said to me, arching his eyes a little, as if telling me to behave. "Mr. Knight, this is Noelle Burrier. She runs the concession stand here."

"Nice to meet you." Mr. Knight held out his hand, giving me an obvious once over. "Are you okay?"

"Yes, I…" It was a little hard to formulate a response when you were looking at one of the most intense people you'd ever met, especially a really good-looking one, but I managed to shake his hand. "I had a little ketchup accident," I finally said. "Which is why I was in the shower when everything happened."

"It's incredibly dangerous for you to be at the arena by yourself this late at night," he said, his hazel eyes never leaving mine.

Why did he look familiar? And why were my hands a little clammy?

"I close by myself all the time," I protested.

"Well, I don't foresee that continuing in the future," he said.

My heart sank, but he'd already turned to Dwayne. "Can you schedule a staff meeting for the day after tomorrow? I was thinking around noon and I can—"

"Most of the employees are teenagers," I interrupted. "They're at school during the day so they wouldn't be able to meet at that time until the weekend. But on weekends, we have hockey games all day, so most of them are busy."

He cocked his head slightly. "So when would you propose a meeting?"

"I don't know," I admitted. "We've never had one before."

"You've never had a staff meeting?" He looked confused.

"Not really. At least, not in the five years I've worked there."

"The arena will be closed tomorrow since we have no way to resurface the ice," he said. "But the new Zamboni arrives the day after and I was planning to be here anyway. Can the two of you meet me here around ten and at least give me a tour of the place?"

Dwayne and I briefly glanced at each other and then I nodded. "Sure. I'll be here checking inventory and cleaning up the mess anyway."

"Well, I appreciate it." Mr. Knight looked like he was going to say something else but didn't.

I started tapping my foot because I'd begun to get cold. Even with Dwayne's jacket, wearing slides with no socks on the last day of November was never a good idea here in Garland Grove. Located at the base of a mountain, we got wind gusts that were scary year-round, and winters were brutal. I desperately needed socks. And closed-toe shoes. A warm blanket to curl up in would be nice too.

"Well, I guess I'm going to go," I said finally, though I had no idea where I was going. "Looks like the crowd is dispersing and I can get to my car now."

"You look like you're freezing," Mr. Knight told me. "Go ahead and head home. I'll see you day after tomorrow and we can get to know each other while I get a feel for things here."

"Yes. Thank you. Good night." I nodded, picked up my duffel and turned toward the employee lot in the back.

I unlocked the door of my twelve-year-old Toyota RAV4 and got in, immediately starting the engine and turning on the heat. I didn't drive it much, so it was in good shape for an older vehicle, but I knew from experience it wasn't the most comfortable place to sleep. Especially since the back seat and the trunk area were stuffed to the gills with all my things.

I rubbed my hands together and blew on them to warm them up

faster and finally pulled out my phone. I hated to intrude on anyone, but tonight I had no choice, so I dialed my best friend's number.

"Hey!" Connie Raines answered, sounding out of breath.

"Hey." I paused. "I need a favor."

"Of course."

"Can I crash on your couch tonight?"

"Sure. What's going on?"

"I'll tell you when I get there. Can I come over now?"

"I'm here—Alexander, you take your sister's bottle again and you're going on time-out for the rest of your life!"

"I'll see you in a few." I disconnected and blew out a breath, turning toward the highway. It was forty miles to Connie's house, but at least it was warm and welcoming.

———

I woke up to something cold and wet against my cheek and I jumped, flailing my arms. Connie and her fiancé's border collie, Holtby, yelped in surprise and I sat up, shaking my head.

"Sorry, buddy, but you scared the crap out of me."

Obviously forgiven, Holtby ambled back over and nudged me with his nose. I pet him for a moment before five-year-old Alexander came skidding into the room.

"Mommy says breaksist is ready!" he yelled, leaving as quickly as he'd come.

I yawned and sat up. Their couch wasn't the most comfortable in the world, but it was better than the floor or my car, and it was definitely warm in here. I hadn't slept so well, or for eight straight hours, since the last time I'd slept over. Usually, I only came for the holidays, and Connie would insist I spend the night. She'd told me I could sleep here whenever I needed to, but I didn't want to intrude. She and her fiancé, Craig, had been together about a year-and-a-half and their baby, Daphne, was six months old. They also had Connie's son Alexander, from a previous relationship, so they had enough going on without me crashing on their couch, and anyway, I was too embarrassed to admit I had nowhere else to go.

"Morning." Connie grinned over at me as I entered the kitchen, Daphne in her arms as she put a plate of eggs down in front of Alexander.

"Morning." I poured myself a cup of coffee as Connie quickly and efficiently fed the baby and helped Alexander.

"So, you want to tell me what's going on? I was too tired to hear the story last night." She glanced up at me.

I shook my head. "Same shit, different day." I took a sip of coffee. "Down on my luck and strapped for cash. You know how it is."

She cocked her head. "I thought things were okay?"

"They are." I looked away, hoping she wouldn't press me for details but knowing she would.

"Noelle."

"Connie, there's nothing you can do—you and Craig have your own problems. Don't worry about me. I appreciate you letting me crash on the couch. I might need one more night, but then I'll be okay."

"What aren't you telling me?"

"Remember when Craig lost his second job in three months?" I asked her. "How ashamed you were to admit you were pregnant, again, and involved with another guy who couldn't keep a job? Remember how you didn't want to talk about it?"

"Did you lose your job?" she whispered.

"No, but there's a new owner and rumor has it that he's in town so he can sell the arena. On top of that, the Zamboni caught on fire last night, so it's out of commission, which means we may not have hockey games for a while, and that means we could all be out of a job soon."

"Why didn't you tell me?"

"I just found out yesterday and the fire was last night."

"You've been sleeping at the arena again," she said softly. "That's why you needed to come here last night. You couldn't stay there after a fire and it's too cold to sleep in your car. Oh, Noelle."

I sighed. "I really don't want to talk about it."

"I thought things were fine with Jasmine?"

Jasmine was my old roommate.

"They were. Until she moved her boyfriend in and kicked me out. I didn't have enough money saved for a security deposit and first month's rent on a new place, so I went back to sleeping in my car or on the floor in the storeroom at the arena last summer."

"Last summer?" Connie stared at me. "And you couldn't come to me?"

"You live in a one-bedroom apartment with two kids! What are you going to do with me beyond the occasional night on the couch? It's okay, Con. I'm fine. It's just a little stressful sometimes."

"Leave Garland Grove and move to Vancouver," she said. "That's what we're going to do if Craig can't find something solid soon."

"If I can't afford a place here in Garland Grove, how am I going to afford anything in a big city like Vancouver?"

"Maybe we could get a place together, a three-bedroom, and if you pay a third of the rent and utilities, we can all afford it. What do you think?"

"I think a three-bedroom apartment in Vancouver is a pipe dream." I nibbled on a piece of toast I'd just buttered. "Not to mention, Craig doesn't like me."

"You don't like him either, and he knows it. It's hard on a man's pride when his fiancée's best friend calls him a loser."

"I know. I'm sorry. I guess that's the pot calling the kettle black, eh?"

She shook her head. "You're both so hard on yourselves. You've had some horrible luck since university and so has Craig. The accident at the factory wasn't his fault but he couldn't work for months, until his leg healed. And then he couldn't pass his physical in time for the opening at the tinsel factory so now he's been taking temp work. At least he's trying. He's out there hustling every day. Are you?"

I bristled. "I work sixty hours a week, at least ten of which is unpaid because stuff has to get done whether they pay me or not! I'm at work seven days a week."

"That's not hustling. That's surviving. If you were hustling, you'd be looking for something better. Then you could get back on your feet a lot faster." Connie put the baby in her bouncy seat and walked over to me. "I love you. You know that. But you can't expect things to get better if you don't make some changes. You know what they say about expecting a different outcome when you keep doing the same thing."

"I'm not insane," I said, scowling at her.

"But you've given up. Instead of fighting to get ahead, you've resigned yourself to your fate. And you're better than that."

I got up and walked over to the sink, rinsing out my coffee mug, trying to think about how to answer since I knew Connie wasn't intentionally trying to hurt my feelings. "I haven't given up. I'm going to make a thousand dollars coaching the five-year-old hockey camp the week between Christmas and New Year's, which will help get me into a new apartment. I've also applied to work in the cafeteria at the high school and they said it probably won't happen this year, but one of the women there is retiring at the end of the school year, so next fall I should be all set."

Good jobs in Garland Grove were scarce and affordable housing was expensive, but I would be able to get a small apartment somewhere by midsummer. I had a plan, a budget, and was saving every penny I could, so there was a light at the end of the tunnel. Hopefully, it wouldn't turn out to be another train.

CHAPTER THREE

Remy

The fire hadn't been too bad, and the only thing that wasn't fixable or cleanable was the Zamboni, but while insurance would cover it, we wouldn't be able to use either of the rinks until it was replaced. The new one I'd ordered, which was arriving today, would get them running again but I wasn't sure what to do next. The whole reason I'd come here was to see what kind of shape the arena was in so I could sell it. The fire was an unexpected issue and I couldn't just hire a realtor and get rid of it. Well, I could, but somehow it didn't feel quite so black and white now that I was here.

I'd also been annoyed to see that there was no management team in place and no one that was truly in charge. I had wonderful memories of the outdoor rink as a child, but now everything about the place seemed old and outdated. And while it didn't have to be my problem, it kind of was. Not just because I technically owned it now, but because being back in Garland Grove suddenly brought back so many memories. Memories of a time when my parents had been happy, when my life had been innocent and carefree. Before heart defects and stressful careers and affairs. My father had the affairs, not me, but they had impacted me in more ways than one. Hell, Kingston and I were both extremely gun-shy when it came to relationships because of our father's infidelities.

It was less so for Ashton since he was still so young and didn't remember a time when our parents had been happy together. Kingston and I did, though, so when news of our father's affairs had come out, it had made us both reluctant about serious relationships. Kingston was the lead singer of one of the biggest rock bands in the world right now, touring the globe, sleeping with everything that moved, and living his best life, so I didn't blame him for wanting to be single. Especially since he was just shy of twenty-eight.

It was a little different for me. At thirty-five, most of my friends were settled and had a house full of kids. I'd had neither the time nor the inclination for that with all my different business ventures, and frankly, most of the women I met were interested in my bank accounts, not me. I also had no intention of being like my father, where I kept a wife and family at home while I traveled the world having fun and enjoying everything life had to offer without them. So I kept my eye on the ball, letting business take precedence over everything else, with the exception of my mother and brothers.

Being back in Garland Grove made me a little wistful, though. I remembered watching my parents skate around that outdoor rink, laughing and kissing, as if there was no place else they wanted to be. Mom said everything changed when I left to go play in the juniors and Dad started traveling for weeks at a time. She was home alone with Kingston and started to resent her husband for leaving her so much. The more she resented him, the less often he came home, until there wasn't anything left between them. Not even after Ashton was born.

Thinking about my own lifestyle, I was determined not to repeat those mistakes. I did want to be a dad someday, though, so that made everything complicated. There wasn't anyone special in my life and with how busy I was in general, there probably wouldn't be. I shouldn't have even come to Garland Grove. Fiona had been sending me reminder after reminder of things I had to do, yet here I was about to tour an arena I didn't even want.

If I was honest with myself, there was no reason to have this meeting. I could put a few thousand into upgrading the arena and then put the damn place on the market. Instead, I wanted to know everything about it. It made no sense, but being in Garland Grove reminded me of a time I thought I'd forgotten. Of love and family and—oh, what the fuck was wrong with me?

I shook my head to clear it, reminding myself I wasn't going to stay. There was no reason to get caught up in whatever was going on here in Garland Grove when I was just going to leave.

Except I was *already* involved. I owned this arena and the fire the night before last had been jarring. The idea of it burning to the ground had bothered me, and then once I got here, there had been something about Noelle that had given me pause. I couldn't put my finger on it because at the time she'd looked cold, wet, and terrified. As if there was something beyond the fire that scared her. I'd built my entire career by trusting my gut, from ice hockey to business deals, and my gut told me she needed help. I just didn't know what kind or if I could be the one to provide it.

Tall blonds with green eyes were a bit of a weakness of mine, and green-eyed blonds that were in trouble got me every time. I was a care-taker at my core, whether it was protecting my teammates on the ice, making sure my employees had good benefits, or spending a fuck-ton of money ordering a Zamboni for an ice rink I'd only owned for five minutes. I didn't know if this was a good thing or not, but it made my mom proud and I'd gotten rich along the way, so it couldn't be all bad either.

I spotted Noelle the moment she came down the hall, a duffel bag in her hand. She smiled and waved, approaching me casually. It occurred to me she and everyone else who worked here probably needed their jobs, so they all had to be wondering if I was going to sell the place.

And I was.

Wasn't I?

"Good morning. I brought coffee and bagels. Is there somewhere we can put it?"

"Sure. The family lounge is comfortable and there are tables in there." She started walking back in the direction she'd come from and I took a moment to appreciate her very shapely jean-clad backside.

Stop it, I admonished myself.

"What's the family lounge?" I asked her, picking up the coffee tray and the bags of bagels and spreads.

"It's a heated room with couches, tables, and Wi-Fi, where parents can sit while their kids play or have practice."

"Does the arena stay busy with hockey leagues?"

She nodded. "Oh, yeah. That's our main source of income, as far as I know. I mean, open skating does well on Saturday afternoons, and the outdoor rink is busy seven days a week in December and January, but that's about it."

"Can you give me a basic rundown of how many people work here?" I asked, setting the coffee tray and bags down on a coffee table that had seen better days.

"We have six teenagers who work as ice guards during open skating, and one of them is also a ref for the kids' games, but the other refs just donate their time. They aren't employees. So that's six. Then there's

Dwayne, the maintenance guy you met the other night. Tandy is Dwayne's wife and she works the front desk on the weekends, answering phones and stuff. And there's a guy who does upkeep on the ice, Clarence, but he just comes and goes as necessary, checking the ice."

"What about concession stand employees?"

She shook her head. "Just me. During Christmas break, spring break, whenever we're super busy, some of the ice guards come in for extra shifts to help out but mostly it's just me." Noelle met my gaze hesitantly, as if worried about my response.

"Oh. Okay." The staffing sounded like a clusterfuck, but I didn't want to get off on the wrong foot, so I didn't say anything else for a minute.

"Are you firing us?" she asked after a moment.

"Not at all," I replied smoothly. "I just want to get a feel for how you guys do things, meet all of you, and see if there's anything I can do to make the rink better."

"Give us a Zamboni that doesn't catch fire," she quipped, chuckling.

I laughed. "It'll be here later today."

"How did you get one so fast?" she asked.

"Being a former pro doesn't hurt," I said. "Paying a fuck-ton for expedited shipping helped too."

"I appreciate it," Noelle said, looking right at me, her green eyes filled with sincerity. "Some of us depend on our jobs to survive, so if the rink had been shut down for even a short period of time, it would've been problematic in more ways than one."

"That's why I expedited the shipping," I said quietly.

"So you're *not* going to sell it?" Noelle asked, her eyes meeting mine in what I could only describe as a silent plea.

I hesitated because I didn't want to lie to her, but I also didn't know what I was going to do yet. "I'd like to hear about the hockey program, the open skating schedule, and anything else of importance before I make the final decision. I looked on the website but didn't see any info."

"None of us know how to access the website," Noelle admitted. "I tried but whoever set it up didn't leave us passwords."

"I can hire some tech people to handle that," I said. "Seriously, what else needs fixing, updating, whatever? I want to help. Even if I do decide to sell it, I'll get more money for it if it's in good shape and making a profit."

"We need a skate sharpening machine," she said hesitantly. "Ours is broken and a lot of the kids don't know where else to go to get their skates sharpened."

I made a note on my phone to go with the other dozen or so notes that I'd already sent to Fiona.

"Why don't you tell me why you're here," she said as we settled in two chairs across from each other. "The real reason. I'm an adult, Mr. Knight. I can handle the truth and I would appreciate honesty because there aren't a lot of job prospects here in Garland Grove. If I lose this one, I'll probably have to move."

I grimaced. "Please call me Remy. And everything I've told you has been true. The backstory is pretty simple. I played ten seasons in the NHL before finding out I have a heart defect that forced me to retire. I built a sporting goods empire because I didn't know what else to do with my time, and now I've officially bought an NHL expansion team, so I'm busy *as fuck*. When I found out I'd inherited this arena after my father's will was read, I figured I'd sell it, but I wanted to come check it out first. Now that I'm here, I realize there's a bit of nostalgia involved. I learned to skate here at this arena when I was a kid. My family used to come here for the holidays every year, so I do have a few sentimental reasons for wanting to see it succeed. I'd been here a couple of hours when I heard about the fire so now I guess I'm invested. It doesn't make a lot of sense, not even to me, but that's the truth."

"Sorry I'm late!" Dwayne came running in. "Had to take my kid to school and got a flat on the way back."

"No problem. Have some coffee." I motioned to the coffee and bagels on the table.

"Thanks." He sat down, poured himself a cup and started digging through the bagels.

"Remy was just telling me about how he used to come here as a kid," Noelle told him.

"I remember," Dwayne said, smiling. "It was a big deal when you got drafted and mentioned learning to skate in Garland Grove."

I smiled. "I have good memories here."

"But now you want to sell it."

"Wow, the rumor mill is busy here." I met his gaze. "But I honestly haven't decided anything yet.

"I work two jobs, Mr. Knight, and I need both of them to support my family." Dwayne didn't blink.

I nodded. "I get it, and I'm serious when I say I don't want to hurt anyone no matter what I decide. The truth of the matter is that I don't have time to run a hockey arena in Garland Grove, so if I don't sell it, I need a trusted staff in place. And I don't see much staff at all."

"I don't know much about the finances," Dwayne said, scratching his salt-and-pepper goatee. "But my understanding is that this place doesn't turn enough of a profit to pay anyone else full-time, like a manager or whatever."

I frowned. "But who does the money go to now?"

Dwayne shrugged. "I couldn't tell you."

"I'll get in touch with my attorney," I said. "This is information I need. In the meantime, tell me what *you* need to make your lives easier here."

The suggestions and ideas started coming and kept coming, and I felt bad that they'd operated with the bare minimum of supplies, staff, and amenities for so long. It was amazing the arena was able to continue offering hockey programs and open skating with this level of disorganization. Somehow, whether I sold it or kept it, I needed to find a way to help these people. Not because I had to, but because I suddenly really wanted to.

CHAPTER FOUR

Noelle

I'd been prepared to fight for the arena, my job, and anything else that came up, but there didn't seem to be anything to fight for. Remy wasn't at all what I'd been expecting based on his gruff exterior, and all the arguments I'd prepared had been unnecessary. He seemed attentive, interested, and in no hurry to make a decision about selling the arena. That didn't mean he wouldn't, but it meant I had a chance to talk him out of it.

Despite my personal financial situation, the last thing I wanted to do was leave Garland Grove and move to Vancouver. Sure, I'd probably be able to get a job there, but I loved working at the arena and the idea of sitting behind a desk all day sounded awful. If I got the job at the high school, I'd work there Monday through Friday during the day and run the concession stand a few nights during the week and on weekends. With both jobs, I'd be okay, and I'd still be around hockey and the ice arena I loved.

I'd played hockey in high school and continued to play until a few years ago. Hockey was expensive and I didn't have enough money for a roof over my head, much less a hobby like that. Sometimes I missed it, but mostly I put one foot in front of the other and tried to focus on the future. And right now, my future was dependent upon convincing Remy Knight not to sell the arena.

"We keep it pretty simple back here," I told him as I showed him the concession stand. "I do hotdogs on the weekends or when school's out, but the rest of the time it's mostly soda, candy, and popcorn."

"So on a busy night, how much do you bring in?" he asked, leaning against the counter.

"A couple hundred," I said sadly. "It's kind of a catch-22 because it costs money to bring in other food, like pretzels and nachos, and if they don't sell, it all goes bad and has to be tossed. But without a decent variety, people don't buy as much. If it was my business—" I stopped abruptly and gave him a wry smile. "Sorry. I shouldn't have said anything."

Thick-lashed hazel eyes focused on mine with so much intensity it almost made me dizzy. "No. Please. Finish what you were going to say."

I took a deep breath. "If this were my place, and I was in charge, I'd start out introducing new stuff for free. A lot of the vendors will give you samples if you promise to buy so much in a certain amount of time. So I'd pick a Friday night high school hockey game or something and serve cheeseburgers and fries, for example. Everyone would see how good they are and then the next time there's a game, the burgers would be for sale and hopefully everyone would buy them."

He nodded thoughtfully. "That's a good idea. No one here will let you try?"

"There's no one to ask."

"I keep hearing that and it's really hard to understand. How can there not be anyone in charge?"

"Beats me." I opened the door to the ice machine. "We could really use a repair on this thing. The ice is more big blocks instead of cubes these days, and sometimes it takes me twenty or thirty minutes to break it up."

He peered inside. "Maybe I'll take a look at it later. What else?"

"I could use a raise, if you're offering," I said lightly. "I've worked here five years and have never had an increase in pay or been paid overtime."

He stared at me, squinting slightly. "You've never had a raise and they don't pay you for overtime?"

She shook her head. "When I got hired, right after I graduated from university, I didn't have a lot of job prospects so Mr. Tanner hired me to run the concession stand. I'd played hockey here in high school so—"

He interrupted me. "You play hockey?"

I smiled. "I did. Hockey's an expensive sport and I can't really afford it anymore, but I used to play."

"You work at an ice arena," he protested. "They won't give you a discount or something?"

"Well, yes, but my equipment was destroyed when my last apartment was flooded, and I honestly don't have the money to buy anything new. It's all right. Anyway, Mr. Tanner hired me but he passed away not long after I started, and I don't think anyone's been in charge since then." I paused. "Didn't your father or the attorneys or whoever explain what was what?"

"I didn't even know my father owned the place," Remy said thoughtfully. "I got some financial statements for the arena based on tax returns and such, but there wasn't much other information."

"That seems odd, no?"

"Definitely, but I'm going to get some answers relatively soon. I called my attorney yesterday and he's looking into it ASAP. Frankly, I was supposed to be in Florida getting ready to close on my new house, but I find myself drawn to this place." He looked around almost wistfully. "I don't know why, I just feel compelled to stick around at least a few days and make my decision based on what's best for the arena, the town, and the employees."

I might have fallen a little in love with him in that moment. His hazel-gold eyes were filled with concern as he looked at me and the way he filled out his button-down shirt wasn't bad either. I'd been trying not to stare at his muscular thighs and shapely behind all morning, but it was proving more difficult than I'd anticipated. I hadn't been out on a date in a while and Remy was more than just a little bit attractive. Not that I had any illusions of grandeur with a guy like him, but a girl could fantasize, right?

"You're...*nice*," I said quietly.

"You sound surprised."

"Well, I've heard of you, of course. Both from when you played hockey and now that you're buying the new team in Florida. You seemed larger than life online, like the kind of guy who'd just sell the place sight unseen and keep going with your life. Instead, you came in person and you're...genuine." I needed to stop talking but I couldn't seem to help myself.

"In the interest of full disclosure," he said, a small smile playing on his full lips, "I had no intention of staying. I was going to come by to see it, since I learned to skate here, hire a realtor, and head back out. When the fire happened and I ordered the Zamboni, I realized I wanted to be here to make sure it arrives all right and is what you need, and it seems like with every passing minute, there are more and more unanswered questions. I guess I'm simply not the kind of guy to walk away until I have all the information."

We stared at each other for a minute, a subtle spark igniting between us before I forced myself to look away. "Well, there's plenty of information around here for you to gather. The lights in the men's locker room don't always work, there's no hot water in the showers—it's mostly lukewarm—and the website isn't up to date." I grinned at him, trying to lighten the mood because flirting with him would serve no purpose. Retired pro hockey players like Remy Knight didn't date homeless concession stand managers, and even if he did, he was leaving soon and I had to stay.

"Looks like the Zamboni's here," Dwayne said, turning toward the ice abruptly.

Crap, I'd all but forgotten he was here.

"Excellent." Remy said. "Let's go see this baby."

The three of us grabbed our coffee cups off the concession counter and moved toward the entrance to the ice where the Zamboni would be delivered.

"Oh, it's gorgeous," I breathed, staring at it.

It was brand spanking new, shiny, and white, and would hopefully do a great job resurfacing the ice.

The three of us watched as it was moved off the truck and settled in the area where it would be permanently parked in between ice cleaning.

"Let's gas her up and take her for a spin," Remy said, his eyes twinkling.

"You think?" I wrinkled my nose.

"Well, how else will we test it?" he countered. "And also, it'll be good PR for the rink. I'll put a few pictures up on social media and it'll hopefully get people to come in."

"That's true." I nodded.

"Let's do it." Dwayne and Remy moved off to where they did those types of things—I never paid any attention to putting gas in the Zamboni—and I looked around the ice as if I'd never seen it before. Something about Remy being in the building gave it new life, and while it made no sense, it also made perfect sense. Who else but a former professional hockey player could breathe new life into an old, dilapidated ice arena?

Growing up in Garland Grove, everyone knew the stories about the "magic" of the rink here, especially the outdoor one. We joked about it, but I personally knew half a dozen people who'd fallen in love here at the arena, including Connie. It had never worked for me, so I figured I wasn't the mystical type, but there was definitely a little magic in the air with Remy here. My life was pretty damn boring and a whole lot stressful, but I could absolutely enjoy hanging out with Remy for a couple of days. When would I ever have an opportunity like this again?

"Noelle!" Remy was driving the Zamboni, a big grin on his face. "Come ride with me."

My eyes widened. "What? No. That's okay."

"Yes! Come on—Dwayne will take some pictures of us and we'll put them online."

I wrinkled my nose. "I don't need to be online."

"I say you do." He stopped the Zamboni and held out his hand. "Come on up."

Our eyes locked and for the second time today, everything stopped for a moment. Before I even realized what I was doing, I put my hand in his and climbed up the side.

"Isn't this fun?" He scooted over so there was room for me and I looked around, a big grin crossing my face.

"I've never ridden a Zamboni," I said.

"Me either." He grinned back.

"You've never resurfaced the ice before?" I asked, grimacing. "Do you know how?"

"How hard can it be?"

CHAPTER FIVE

Remy

Okay, driving a Zamboni around the ice was harder than it looked. Maybe not hard exactly, but not easy either. I needed some practice before I could make those perfect turns smoothing out the ice. Luckily, we were all having too much fun to care and watching Noelle laugh made me happy. Maybe it was because my life was usually so high-stress I rarely had time to do something as carefree as driving a Zamboni. Or laughing with a green-eyed blond who reminded me it had been a minute or ten since I'd had sex.

Not that I would use Noelle like that, but it was sure fun to imagine her naked. Mostly, though, I imagined her laughing like she was now. Her head thrown back, golden hair flying out behind her. Except in my fantasy, she was naked. And on top of me. Ironically, though, even in the throes of imaginary passion, I still envisioned her smiling. Happy. Somehow, my gut told me she didn't have much of that in her life. There was a sadness in her eyes that was always there, and I longed to ask her about it. The urge to write her a big check and discreetly deposit it in her account was almost overwhelming, and I had no idea why.

"I think this looks pretty good," Dwayne called out. "Now why don't you get down and let me do the outside rink before you hurt yourself?"

I laughed and climbed down, holding out a hand to help Noelle. "That was fun. Sorry if I took ten times longer than I should have."

"Hey, when the boss wants to do my job for me, and all I have to do is take pictures? I'm good." Dwayne was laughing too.

"Probably the first and last time I'll ever do it," I conceded.

"That was really fun," Noelle said, "but I've got to do inventory. Is there anything else you need from me?"

I shook my head. "Not that I can think of. Would you mind if I tagged along, though? I really do want to see how everything works around here."

She hesitated for a fraction of a second, but then nodded, stuffing her hands in her pockets. "Sure. Come on."

I spent the next few hours lifting and moving boxes as Noelle counted every box of candy, canister of soda, package of napkins, and all the other items that filled in the concession stand, as well as the storeroom. I hadn't worked this hard in years and was a little surprised that she did it all on her own.

"How often do you do inventory?" I asked her as we finished up.

"Once a month. I come in early, usually on the first of the month, and get it done. The fire delayed me by a couple of days, but I'll place an order tonight."

"Do you call the vendors directly?"

"We just use one." She gave me the details on the ordering process, and I made a mental note to find out how much money she made. It seemed like she took on a lot of responsibilities and I had a feeling she made very little.

A rumbling in my stomach reminded me it was late in the day and I hadn't eaten anything since that bagel this morning. We'd finally finished inventory and it occurred to me I was going to spend another evening in my room eating takeout and working unless I did something to change my plans.

"Can I take you to dinner?" I asked her impulsively.

She glanced up in surprise, myriad emotions flitting across her face. "Uh...what?"

"I'm sorry," I said quickly. "You probably have a boyfriend. I didn't mean any disrespect. I've just enjoyed your company today."

She fixed those green eyes on me and blinked a couple of times. "I don't have a boyfriend," she said softly, her eyes never leaving mine.

"So...dinner then? My stomach is growling and all I've had since I got to Garland Grove is takeout."

"There are some great restaurants in town; it just depends on what you're in the mood for. I'm not really dressed for anything fancy."

"Doesn't have to be fancy. Is there a pub or some place that has good burgers and beer?"

She grinned. "Absolutely. The Twisted Tinsel Bar. The burgers are great, and the poutine is better."

"Would you like to go?" I looked down at her and she was worrying her lower lip but then a slow smile spread across her face.

"Sure. You want to follow me there?"

"Why don't we go together and I can drop you off back here when we're done?"

She hesitated but then nodded. "Okay."

We walked into what was obviously an older building, with wooden floors and brick walls. There were far too many neon signs, but somehow they made it bright and homey, instead of dark and dank, like a lot of bars I'd been to this size. I had my hand at the small of Noelle's back as we walked in and an older guy behind the bar looked up, narrowing his eyes slightly as he made no secret of the fact he was checking me out.

"Hey, Noelle." He eyed me. "Dinner, drinks, or both?"

"Both," I replied, meeting his gaze.

He came out from around the bar and put two menus down in front of us.

"Hi, Horace." Noelle smiled up at the guy. "This is Remy—"

"Knight." Horace nodded. "You were a hell of a player back in the day."

I inclined my head politely. "Thank you."

"Damn shame it ended so soon, but it's good to see you're doing well."

"I appreciate that."

"Can I get you a drink?"

"Molson Canadian, please."

"Noelle?" Horace asked her.

She smiled. "Since I'm not driving, how about one of your special eggnogs?"

He winked. "Coming up."

He walked away and I picked up the menu. "What do you recommend?"

"The poutine is awesome—best in town. The burgers are big and filling."

"A burger and poutine on the side," I said, closing the menu.

She chuckled. "Will you share your poutine with me if I get a burger too?"

"Absolutely."

Horace brought our drinks and we placed our dinner orders. I kept my burger simple, with cheddar cheese, lettuce and tomato. Noelle ordered it with everything—including bacon and pickles.

"Mmm, this is good." Noelle took a sip of her drink. "Strong, but good. Wanna try it?"

"Sure." I took the proffered glass and took a sip. It was a little sweet for me, but strong and tasty. "Excellent. Are you not a beer drinker?"

She shrugged. "I can be, but not usually. This is much yummier." She took another sip.

"So what do you do when you're not working?" I asked her.

"Not a lot. I go to the library and sometimes I hang out with my bestie, Connie, but she's engaged and has two kids so she doesn't have a lot of free time. I come here once in a while to watch a hockey game since I don't have cable."

"Who's your team?"

She lifted her palms, eyeing me as if I were daft. "Come on, really? Vancouver. Duh."

I chuckled. "That's fair."

"What's *your* favorite team?" she countered.

I grinned. "The Lauderdale Knights. *Duh.*"

"You got me." Her smile lit up her whole face. "But what was it *before* you bought your own team? You had to have a favorite growing up."

"Of course. I was born and raised in Vancouver, so..."

She threw back her head and laughed. "That's awesome."

"Here we are." Horace arrived with our food and I had to admit it looked amazing. The burger was freakin' huge and the poutine made my mouth water a little. I had a feeling the Canadian specialty wouldn't be easy to find in Fort Lauderdale, so I figured I'd better enjoy it while I could.

"So when are you leaving?" Noelle asked and then promptly clapped a hand over her mouth. "I'm sorry—I didn't mean it to sound like that!"

I laughed. "It's fine. But I don't know yet. I thought I'd already be gone. Instead, I keep sending my assistant emails asking her to do this or that for the rink."

"What I meant was, do you have a bunch of stuff to handle in Fort Lauderdale?"

"I do, but nothing important until after the first of the year. My attorney is doing the closing on my new house, and that was the only pressing thing on my agenda."

"What about your wife or girlfriend?" she asked. "Isn't she there?"

I lifted my eyes to hers. "You think I'd be out on a date with you if I had a wife or girlfriend?"

Her cheeks turned pink. "Is this a...date?"

"I asked you to go out to dinner and you said yes. Is that not the definition of a date?"

"I wasn't sure, I guess. I thought maybe just a business dinner kind of thing."

"Do most guys ask you to go out for business dinners?" I asked curiously.

She shook her head. "No. I don't date a lot these days. It's exhausting."

"Exhausting? That's not a word I usually associate with dating."

"Because you're a guy. It's different for women. Like, sex is fine. I'm not easily offended so if I go out on a date and he wants to get naked, depending on the guy and my mood, I might say yes or no. But the issue comes if it's no. Then there's the cajoling. The whining. The eventual frustration or anger. It's like a whole ordeal because maybe I'm just tired or I'm on my period, or frankly, the guy turned out to be super boring and annoying. Eventually, you get to the point where it's easier not to date."

"Yet here we are."

"Yup. Here we are." She looked up at me, her eyes burning into mine.

"Am I super boring or annoying?"

"Not yet."

I winked. "Give me a few minutes."

CHAPTER SIX

Noelle

We talked until long after we'd finished eating. I wound up having a second eggnog, which made me tipsy as hell, but that was okay. I wasn't driving and alcohol would help me sleep better since I'd be back on the floor of the locker room tonight. I had an air mattress but it was hard sneaking it out of the arena in the morning unless I got up super early. Dwayne already suspected I slept there more than just the once in a while I'd told him I did. Otherwise, it would have been a lot more comfortable to sleep on the couch in the lounge. It was too easy to get caught there, though, so I'd gotten creative.

"Why do you look sad all of a sudden?" Remy was asking me.

"Oh, I wasn't sad," I said quickly. "Just thinking of all the work I've got coming up when the candy order arrives."

"You really need help," he said slowly. "That's one of the things on my list to do tomorrow. Once I figure out who, exactly, is handling the finances, I'm going to hire some new people. I've already got a plan in my head."

"How did you go from hockey to business?" I asked curiously.

"Do you know what happened to me?" he asked.

"You had a heart attack on the ice," I said softly. "I can't imagine what that was like. You must have been terrified."

"Honestly, I don't remember much. I remember feeling weird and telling one of my teammates I needed to get to the bench. The next thing I remember is waking up in the hospital."

I nodded. "Still. Your family, friends...watching that on TV or if they were there..."

"My mother saw it on TV," he said. "She said she was hysterical, calling my dad immediately, even though they were legally separated at the time."

"That would be awful for a mom. For anyone who cares about you, but mostly a mom."

"Luckily, I'm okay. I had to retire from hockey, but that's better than the alternative. Anyway, I needed something to do while I was essentially relegated to bed rest and I started talking to a buddy of mine who'd done a bunch of endorsements. He gave me some ideas, so I got on the phone with my agent, and pretty soon I'd filmed a few commercials and started building a life away from hockey. I didn't know at that point whether or not I'd have to retire, but I had a feeling. Deep down, I knew that after major heart surgery, I might not come back, and I had to be prepared."

"Do you miss it?" I asked. "Hockey, I mean?"

"Every damn day. So much I bought my own team. I figure that should keep me immersed in hockey day in and day out." His eyes twinkled.

"Sounds reasonable. I get my hockey fix by working at the arena, I guess."

"Time for some new equipment, eh? Is there a women's team?"

I shook my head. "No, but most of the beer league teams are coed."

"Would you play if you had equipment?"

"I can't afford the fees. It's a lot and I'm saving up for an—a new apartment, because where I am now really sucks."

"Can I help?" he asked. "Maybe make some calls to find you a better place or give you a reference of some kind as your employer?"

"I appreciate it, but I'm good. Hopefully I'll have the money by next summer and things will be easier."

He seemed thoughtful for a moment before asking, "Would you like to take a walk? The Christmas decorations on Main Street seemed pretty as we were driving here."

"Sure." It was probably a dumb idea, because I wasn't dressed for the cold weather, but spending a little more time with him sounded too good to refuse. This might be my one and only date with him and I wanted to enjoy every second of it.

Remy paid the bill, shook Horace's hand, and we headed outside.

The temperature had dropped drastically and there was a cold wind blowing.

"Is it too cold?" Remy asked, glancing down at me.

"Maybe a little, but once we start to walk I'll be okay."

"Do you have gloves?"

"Not with me. I didn't know we were going to be outside."

"Here." He took his off and handed them to me. "I'm fine."

"Thank you." I wasn't going to refuse, even though I wanted to, because it was freakin' freezing out and he was being sweet. I slid the massive gloves, which were warm from his body temperature, onto my hands and they felt so good. I had one good pair of gloves, but they were in my car somewhere since I didn't spend much time outside in the winter.

"Did you say you went to university?" he asked as we walked past a row of shops with brightly decorated lights.

"Yes. I have a degree in hospitality and hotel management."

"No jobs like that around here?"

"Not hardly. I'd have to move to Vancouver, and though I've considered it, it's hard to get started in a new place, especially a big city. I don't know anyone there, and I'd definitely need a roommate to survive, so it's complicated. Small-town life doesn't prepare you for careers and such."

"I'm going over the numbers with my accountant tomorrow," he said. "Once I know all the details, I'm going to try and get raises for both you and Dwayne. You seem to be the only two holding down the fort."

"A raise would be really appreciated—oh look!" I smiled at the huge Christmas tree in the town square. "They just turned on the lights! It wasn't lit up last time I was here."

"It's beautiful." He reached for my hand and tugged me in that direction. "Let's take a selfie."

"Somehow, I didn't picture you as the selfie type," I said, laughing.

"I'm not, but this is as close as I've gotten to a vacation this year, so why not have a little fun?" He slid his arm around my shoulders, lifted his phone and snapped a few pictures. My hair was probably a mess, my makeup had faded throughout the course of the day, and I was tired, but being out with Remy made all my problems seem far away.

"Let me see!" I said, peering at his phone. He pulled up the pictures and I grimaced. "I look awful! Don't post those."

"You look beautiful," he said in a deep voice that gave me goose bumps. "The wind whipping through your hair, your smile almost as bright as the lights of the tree...why would you want to look any different?"

"I..." My voice trailed off because I wasn't sure what to say about that. "I don't, I guess, but I would've liked to add a little lip gloss or something."

He gazed down at me, his hazel eyes turning into liquid gold as he studied my face. "You're beautiful just the way you are, Noelle."

Oh, shit, he was going to kiss me. I hadn't brushed my teeth in something like fifteen hours and I was a little tipsy from those two special eggnogs, but when his lips grazed mine, none of it mattered. It was the sweetest, most sensual kiss ever, and he wasn't even trying to stick his tongue down my throat. Just the lightest touch of his lips moving over mine had my heart kicking into gear and my eyes fluttering closed. How was something so chaste hotter than the summer sun?

Suddenly, I wasn't cold anymore. Cold was the exact opposite of what I was feeling right now.

"Ah, you're sweet," he murmured, pulling away. "But it's freezing out here and you're shivering. We should get going."

He wrapped one of his hands around mine and we walked back toward Twisted Tinsel, which was where he'd parked.

"Can I take you out on another date, Noelle?" he asked once we were in his rental SUV and the heat was turned up high.

"Yes." Saying no would be stupid. Even if I was nothing more than a short-term distraction for him while he was here in Garland Grove, when else would I ever date a retired professional hockey player? On top of that, he was a gentleman, and it had been a long time since I'd dated one of those.

"Where would you like to go? And when?"

"I'll be working Friday and Saturday nights, so maybe Sunday? We could go to the holiday bazaar. It's kind of like a flea market, but with lots of new stuff and local crafts, mostly geared toward holiday gifts."

"Sounds fun. And then dinner?"

"Sure." I nodded as he pulled into the back parking lot of the arena.

"I'm over there," I said, motioning to my RAV4.

"Okay." He pulled up alongside it and then turned to me. "Thanks for going out with me tonight. I had a good time."

"Me too." I swallowed, wondering if he was going to kiss me again.

"I'll stop by the arena tomorrow and say hello. What time do you start?"

I hesitated, really hating that I had to lie to him—and everyone else

—about my life. "I'm not sure, probably late morning or early afternoon."

"Well, give me your number and I can text you."

"Okay." We exchanged numbers and I reluctantly got out of the vehicle.

"See you tomorrow, Noelle," he said softly, his eyes never leaving mine.

"Good night. See you tomorrow." I hurried to my car, wondering if he was going to sit and wait for me to leave or if he'd just take off.

Of course, he wasn't going to take off.

I sighed and started the engine. I'd have to drive around the block a few times until I was sure he was gone. Then I'd come back to the arena and try to get some sleep.

CHAPTER SEVEN

Remy

I spent most of the next day on the phone. The Garland Grove Arena was a hot fucking mess and it took my attorney, my accountant, my assistant and myself to figure out the financial situation. My father, in his infinite wisdom and hands-off approach to pretty much everything, had hired a financial firm to handle bills, payroll, and taxes. Tandy made weekly deposits while credit card transactions went directly to the financial firm.

The reason no one got raises was because no one turned in hours or time sheets. Whoever set up payroll had literally been told to pick an amount and cut paycheques for that amount until told otherwise. And there was no one to tell them otherwise.

Frustration shot through me as I looked at how much, or rather, how *little*, Noelle made. She was never going to be able to rent a decent apartment on this kind of money. I didn't know where she lived now but with a salary this low, I couldn't figure out how she survived at all. No wonder she didn't have a decent coat or gloves.

Though my laptop was open in front of me, I was no longer focused on the information. In fact, all I'd thought about since yesterday was Noelle. Last night's kiss hadn't been planned, and though I was sure she would've let me kiss her again at the end of the night, I'd opted not to. It was probably a little bit of a dick move on my part, sending her mixed messages, but she wasn't the kind of woman you used for a few weeks of sex until you moved on. And I was leaving soon so I didn't want to make her life anymore complicated than it already was. She didn't say much, but every instinct I had told me she needed help.

That she needed money was a given, but there was more to it and even after just a couple of days, she intrigued me like no one had in a long time. I wanted to spend every minute of my time in Garland Grove with her, but that would be incredibly selfish. I probably should have just left her alone, worked behind the scenes to get her a raise, and minded my own business. But that protective part of me came out in full force every time we were in the same room together and I didn't know what to do about it.

When I got to the arena the next day, there were a ton of cars in the parking lot. It was just after six and there was a high school hockey game at seven that I was interested in watching, but mostly I wanted to see Noelle. I'd dressed in jeans, a hoodie, and a baseball cap to keep my identity somewhat hidden because I didn't want to cause a scene that would detract from the hockey teams that were playing.

I went down the concourse toward the concession stand and was shocked to see a line with at least fifty people. Noelle was there by herself, and I picked up my pace, hurrying over to her and sliding behind the counter.

"What can I do?" I asked automatically.

"Hi." She was sweaty and a little breathless. "Put on a pair of gloves. I need four hotdogs. Buns are in the warmer over there."

I looked around, unsure where to start, but I saw the box of gloves and put on a pair after I washed my hands. It took about thirty seconds of fumbling around, but I finally figured out where everything was and that tongs were a much better way to pick up hotdogs right off the grill.

I was amazed at how efficient Noelle was. She handled each customer without missing a beat, calling out to me when she needed hotdogs, bottled water, or popcorn, while she filled fountain drinks and candy orders. And then just like that it was over. By five after seven, when the game started, there was no one else in line and we were sold out of hotdogs and Reese's Peanut Butter Cups.

"Holy shit." I just stared at her. "You do this by yourself every night?"

"It's not usually this busy," she said, wiping down the counter. "But tonight is a big rivalry game, so we're busier than usual because of that."

"Will it get busy again between periods?"

"Yes, but not like just now. That was the big rush. They'll be back for drinks and maybe some more candy, but that's it for hotdogs and popcorn."

I glanced over at the countertop grill. "There's not a single hotdog left. Do you always guess how many you're going to sell?"

"Usually there's three or four still left because I hate to have to turn anyone away, but tonight was busier than I anticipated."

"Do you start cleaning up now?"

"I try to clean as I go. The game will be over around nine and then there's a men's league game at ten so I hang out a little while in case they want water or anything."

"Do you *have* to hang around?"

Her eyes met mine questioningly. "Well...no, I guess not. Why?"

"Let's go get a late dinner. I enjoyed spending time with you last night and I'd like to get to know you better. If you're interested." I couldn't remember the last time a woman made me feel a little unsure about my next move. They were usually practically foaming at the mouth to get a second date, yet Noelle seemed hesitant.

"It'll probably be close to ten before I can get out of here," she said finally.

"That's okay. I had a late lunch." I paused. "Did you have dinner already?"

"No, I've been here since noon."

"Perfect."

We went back to the Twisted Tinsel Bar since it was late and neither of us were dressed to go anywhere nicer. Horace greeted us like old friends, immediately bringing me a Molson and an eggnog for Noelle.

"Food or just drinks tonight?" he asked us.

"Food." We spoke in unison and then smiled at each other.

"The fish and chips are on special tonight," Horace said. "You should try it."

"Two," I replied, after Noelle gave me a little nod.

"That was easy," she said, smiling.

"Horace seems to take good care of his customers."

"He's been here for a long time. He knows everyone and everything that goes on in town."

"I'm not sure if that's reassuring or terrifying."

She smiled. "Horace is a good guy."

"Oh, I meant to ask you earlier." I pulled out my phone. "How would you like to go to Vancouver to see the Vipers play? I can get tickets for Tuesday night."

"Oh!" Her eyes widened. "Really? Doesn't hockey…bore you?"

I burst out laughing. "Really? I just bought an entire *team* because I missed it so much. Believe me, hockey never bores me."

"Then, yes, I'd like to go. Very much."

"I'll get the tickets."

Our food arrived and we talked about all kinds of things as we ate. She was funny and well-read, but I noticed she didn't talk about herself much. She told me about her friend Connie's kids, funny things that happened at the arena, and that she'd been a right wing when she played hockey. Beyond that, she kept the conversation light and deflected whenever I asked her anything personal.

"Are your parents still alive?" I asked her once we'd finished eating.

She shook her head. "My mom is, but I never knew my dad. He left when I was a baby. Mom moved to the States to take care of her mother when I turned eighteen."

"You didn't want to go?"

"She didn't ask." She finished the rest of her eggnog in one big gulp. "We're not close."

"I'm sorry."

"Are you close to your mom?"

"Yup. And my brothers too."

"That sounds nice. I'm an only child and Mom, well, she's difficult. She essentially blames me for my dad leaving. Like I'm the one who got pregnant and had me."

"Parents can be difficult. My dad and I weren't close either. And now he's gone."

"Do you regret not working harder to have a better relationship now that he's passed away?"

"Not really. Once he and Mom officially separated, he kind of separated from us kids too. I was already an adult and Kingston was in college, but it was still hard. When I had the heart attack and we found out it was genetic, I immediately had the boys—my brothers—tested. Luckily, they're okay, but Dad refused, saying he'd been fine for nearly sixty years and the tests wouldn't change anything."

"You can't save people who don't want to be saved."

"No, you can't. I do work harder at staying in touch with my mom and brothers, though. Kingston's on tour and Ashton's in college, so it's not easy, but we try to meet up for Christmas, birthdays, whenever we can."

"Are you going home for Christmas?"

"My mom is still in Vancouver, so yes, I'll be home for Christmas.

Ashton too. We're not sure about Kingston, but he said he's trying to work it out."

"The last Christmas I spent with my mom, she drank until she passed out and told me she forgot to buy me anything."

"Your mom sounds lovely," I muttered, unable to hide my annoyance.

"Just gives me a goal, you know?"

"A goal?"

"The kind of mother I don't want to be if I ever become one."

CHAPTER EIGHT

Noelle

I wasn't sure what his reaction would be to me talking about having kids, but his face was serious as he nodded.

"Ditto. About the kind of father I don't want to be."

"Do you want kids?"

"I do." He nodded slowly. "With the right woman, and definitely not in the next year while I get this new team off the ground, but yeah. I can't wait to do all the things my—" He was cut off by the loud ringing of my phone. Connie's name flashed on the screen, and I frowned. It was late, especially for her.

"I'm sorry," I said. "My friend Connie never calls this late—hang on. Con?"

"Oh thank god." Connie sounded frantic.

"What's wrong?"

"A pipe burst and I can't reach the landlord. A plumber won't even come out without giving them a credit card number and we don't have one anymore."

"I don't either," I said miserably. "Where's Craig? Can't he do something?"

"He's not here and I can't reach him either." Connie sounded panicked. "There's water everywhere and the baby's crying...I don't know what to do!" She burst into tears.

"Con, I don't know what to do either. Without a credit card—"

"I have a credit card," Remy interrupted me. "What do you need?"

His gaze was calm and steady, and he put one of his big, warm hands over one of mine, but I couldn't let him get involved.

"I…" I cleared my throat. "Con, it'll take me about forty-five minutes to get there, but I'll leave now, okay? We'll figure it out." I disconnected and reached for my purse, giving Remy an apologetic look. "I'm so sorry, but I have to go. Connie's having an issue and she doesn't know where her fiancé is."

"Why do you need a credit card? Let me help."

"I don't know how long it would be before they could pay you back," I said slowly. "It's wonderful of you to offer but—"

"I'm not worried about being paid back. It's the holidays and if someone is struggling, I have the means to help. So let me. Please. It makes me feel good."

"You don't even know Connie," I protested, though the fight had all but left me.

"But I know you and she's obviously important to you."

Here we were with another one of those situations where you had to compromise your principles for common sense. It was freezing cold and if there was water leaking into Connie's apartment, she had those babies to think about. My pride, her pride, no one's pride was going to keep those kids safe and warm.

"There's a leak and water everywhere but she can't reach the landlord and the plumbers she's called need a credit card on file or they won't even make the trip. Neither of us have one."

"Give me her address," he said, pulling out his phone. He started typing something on the keyboard and then motioned to Horace. "Horace—you got a pen and a piece of paper?"

"Sure thing, Remy!" Horace called back, picking up a pen and a small pad from behind the register and bringing it over to us.

"Thanks." Remy looked up at me, the pen in his left hand as he wrote down the address I recited for him.

"You're a leftie," I said absently. "I am too."

"I wonder if two lefties would have kids who were left-handed too?"

"Is it genetic?" I asked.

"I dunno." He grinned. "But I'll look it up after I call this plumber I found."

It took him about fifteen minutes, but he found a plumber willing to go right to Connie's place and I texted her to expect him soon.

"I still think I need to go," I told him. "She'll probably need help with the kids and cleaning up and stuff."

"Okay, let's both go." He grabbed his keys.

"You don't have to come."

"It's freezing out and looks like it's starting to snow. The roads might be slippery."

"I've been driving on slippery roads my entire life," I pointed out.

"Yeah, but it makes me feel macho to pretend I'm taking care of an obviously independent, self-sufficient woman like you." His eyes twinkled with mirth and we both laughed.

We drove to Connie's and despite our banter, it was nice to have someone else in charge. Connie and I were strong, independent women for the most part, but it was hard to be strong or independent when you were broke. Being strong wasn't going to get a plumber out to the apartment. As much as it made me uncomfortable for Remy to be helping Connie, at least it wasn't for me. I wanted to keep my current living situation a secret from him because it was embarrassing enough for a few friends to know, but Remy was a whole other ball game. He would be leaving Garland Grove by Christmas anyway, and if we could have fun together until then, it would be amazing. I didn't want pity, though. And I definitely didn't need a guy to swoop in and save me.

Well, okay, who was I kidding? I did need that, but only it if was someone who loved me and wanted to be with me. Someone like Remy, who was here today and essentially gone tomorrow, would only make me feel bad about myself, and I already felt pretty miserable about the direction my life had taken. The truth was, until I liked myself, how could anyone else? That was something I was working on, but Remy was the first guy I'd clicked with like this in a long time, so the last thing I was going to do was let him know just how down on my luck I was.

"You don't know how much I appreciate this," Connie said for what had to be the tenth time. Remy had found the pipe that burst and turned off the water coming into the apartment, and the emergency plumber would be here any minute.

"It's my pleasure," Remy said, smiling at her.

Damn, he looked good enough to eat with the sleeves of his button-down shirt rolled up to his elbows. His forearms were muscular and veiny, with the edge of a tattoo snaking down and around his left one. His normally slicked-back dark hair was a little unkempt at the moment, a piece falling forward over one eye and making him look younger.

Connie caught me ogling his behind and elbowed me in the ribs as we swallowed down giggles. Not that Remy's ass was a reason to laugh

—it was downright delectable—but the fact that we were acting like schoolgirls with crushes was the most fun we'd had together in years.

The plumber got there as we were trying to sop up the water with towels, and Connie took both kids into her bedroom to try to get them to sleep. Remy talked to and worked with the plumber quietly and efficiently, as if he dealt with leaks all the time, and I finally collapsed on the couch. It had been a long day, and by the time the plumber left, it was three in the morning.

"You look tired," Remy said, sinking down next to me.

"I am. You?"

He nodded. "Yeah, but we should get going since it's about a forty-minute drive."

"That's far at three in the morning. Let's just get a little rest here until morning and then drive back. I can't even keep my eyes open."

He seemed conflicted but then nodded. "I could use a few hours of shut-eye."

"Thank you for coming tonight," I whispered, settling against his side.

"You're welcome." He pressed a soft kiss on the top of my head and then I was asleep.

I woke to a crick in my neck and my bladder screaming for mercy, so I went into the bathroom to relieve myself. Remy was still asleep on the couch where we'd given up trying to be comfortable and just relaxed as best we could. We probably should have driven home but I was worried about Connie and it had been so late. Besides, sleeping curled up on a couch next to Remy was way better than sleeping on the cold, rubber floor mats in the women's locker room at the arena.

"Who the hell are you and what *the fuck* are you doing in my house?!" Craig's voice boomed through the apartment, and I jumped, yanking up my jeans and running out to the living room.

Remy and Craig were nose to nose, Craig's hands balled into fists at his side.

"Connie!" He yelled out her name even louder.

"Jesus fucking Christ, Craig." I hurried next to Remy. "Would you settle down? This is...my boyfriend. We came to help Connie with the leak in the kitchen."

Craig was still shooting daggers at Remy with his eyes and Remy didn't even flinch, but Connie came running into the living room, eyes wide.

"Craig, I swear to god, if you wake the kids..."

"You can't bring a man into my house when I'm not here," he growled. "How did you expect me to respond?"

"I expect you to show a little gratitude since your children and I were standing in four inches of water before Remy and Noelle got here."

"You should've called me."

"I did! At least ten times."

Craig looked startled and then yanked his phone out of his pocket. "It's dead," he muttered. "Damn battery doesn't last for shit."

"We should go," I murmured to Remy, who nodded.

"Thanks for your help," Connie said to us.

"Anytime." I gave her a quick hug and pulled on my boots.

Craig didn't say a word, merely disappeared into the bedroom and Connie stared after him with a sigh. "Sorry," she whispered.

"It's okay." I squeezed her hand. "I'll talk to you later, okay?"

"Thanks again. You too, Remy." She swallowed, looking from me to Remy and back. "Could we, uh, not say anything about who paid the plumber? I'll find a way to pay you back but—"

"Don't worry about it," Remy said quickly. "Really. It was my pleasure. Any friend of Noelle's is a friend of mine."

CHAPTER NINE

Remy

We got into my rental and I turned the heat up. It was six in the morning and I'd had less than three hours of sleep. I couldn't wait to get back to the bed and breakfast and stretch out on a real bed. Three more hours would be plenty. The only question was whether or not I could get Noelle to come with me. I wasn't even particularly interested in sex at this early juncture, but cuddling with her, spending a little time alone would be nice. She was always running off somewhere to do something, and for once, I wanted to just hang out.

"Sorry I had to tell him you were my boyfriend," she said once we were on the road. "It was the easiest way to diffuse the situation."

"No worries. That's what I figured." I reached across the center console for her hand. "So, since we're a couple now, I have a question."

"Hmm?" She was half asleep.

"Want to come back to my place with me and take a nap? I'm serious about the nap too. This isn't some half-assed ploy to get you into bed, because if that was the case, I'd just say that's what I wanted. And let me be clear—I would *very much* like to get you into bed, just not when we're both dead on our feet like we are now."

"I'm twenty-seven," she said, gazing over at me. "This would not be the first time I've slept with a guy without having sex. I'll also be honest and say that I would very much like to see you naked at some point, but you're right, not when we're both exhausted like this. The way I feel right now, I think I'd sleep through it."

"Trust me, sweetheart. If and when that happens, you're not going to sleep through any of it."

"I have no doubt." Her eyes fluttered closed but there was a smile on her lips as she leaned back in the seat.

———

We slept more than three hours. It was almost seven-thirty before we finally got into bed and the next time I looked at my phone, it was noon. Noelle was still fast asleep, snoring softly, and I took a moment to drink in the sight of her in my bed. She looked so young when she slept, her face devoid of makeup and buried in the side of her pillow. She was striking, though, even with those beautiful green eyes closed. Her pink lips were parted softly, and they were curved into the tiniest smile, as if she were dreaming about something nice.

Desire rippled through me.

I really wanted to touch her but even though she'd slept beside me willingly, I'd never assume anything about a woman I was interested in having sex with. Until she was awake enough to give me a green light, I'd have to be happy just watching her sleep. She was sleeping hard, too, as if she didn't sleep enough. I thought she was gorgeous, but there was no mistaking the faint dark circles under her eyes or the wariness in her eyes when I asked her things like where her gloves were. I sensed she didn't have any, but she was cagey about those types of things.

She wasn't letting on how broke she was, but since I wanted to sleep with her, any exchange of money would make that weird. Maybe not in the grand scheme of things since guys gave their girlfriends money all the time, but this was different. She wasn't my real girlfriend and I was leaving town soon.

I was contemplating my next move when she shifted, her eyes fluttering open as she squinted at me.

"Morning," I said softly. "Did I wake you?"

"No." She muffled a yawn and turned onto her back. "What time is it?"

"Just after noon."

"Wow. I never sleep this late."

"You looked like you needed it."

"I don't sleep well in general, so I probably did." She sat up and looked around. "I barely remember getting here."

"Me either. You hungry?"

"I could eat."

"I texted Rudy, the owner here, when I woke up and explained we'd had a family emergency last night, so he agreed to make us breakfast when we got up. What do you think?"

"Sounds awesome. I could use a shower, though."

"Go ahead and take one. I'll take mine later."

"Thank you." She flashed me a sweet smile, grabbed her jeans off the floor and disappeared into the bathroom.

God, I could only imagine what she looked like in there. Naked. Water glistening on her skin. My dick immediately stiffened behind my sweats, and I sighed, forcing myself to think about other things. I'd been too tired to think about seducing her last night but now that we were awake and she was walking around my room, I couldn't think of anything else.

I pulled on jeans and a T-shirt, lamenting the fact that I'd only brought enough clothes for a few days and now I needed to do laundry. Hopefully, I could throw Rudy a few bucks and he'd take care of it for me. Just like he'd agreed to make us a late breakfast after I told him to add whatever he thought was fair to my bill.

Suddenly, I had an idea. I needed clothes and if I asked her to take me shopping then I could find a way to buy her a few things too. It was a half-assed plan that might backfire, but I had to try. Besides, it was the holidays, and I liked doing things for others. It was usually more in the form of charitable donations, but one-on-one was a nice change of pace. I wanted to do something more to help Connie too, and I brought it up at breakfast.

"How bad are things for Connie and Craig?" I asked her once we had steaming plates of eggs and bacon in front of us.

She sighed. "Pretty bad. Craig lost his job when Connie was pregnant and hasn't done much of anything to get back on his feet. They live in subsidized housing, of course, but it's not enough and the last thing they needed was another kid. I mean, Alexander isn't his—Connie had him with her ex—but they shouldn't have had a baby. Craig is one of those guys I just want to shake. I don't know what she sees in him."

"It takes two to tango," he pointed out.

"Absolutely, and Connie has the worst taste in men. Always has. Craig was good with Alexander at first, so she thought she'd finally found the one, and to be fair, he's a nice guy. He's generally kind and gentle with her and the kids, he doesn't hit her or anything—and Alex's father did, so that's a step up—but he can't keep a job and, frankly, any guy who whines about wearing a condom, well, that just pisses me off."

I grimaced. "Really? Unwanted pregnancies and potential diseases are better than wearing a condom?"

She shrugged, popping a piece of biscuit in her mouth before saying, "Seems that way."

"The bare skin type condoms are good," I said, taking a sip of coffee. "I mean, actually bare is better, but not by a ton. And frankly, I can go for a *long* time with a condom—which is always better for the woman."

Her eyes met mine over the rim of her coffee cup. "How long is a long time?" she asked in a slightly raspy voice.

Christ.

My cock sprang to attention and I was glad that the tablecloth covered most of my lap.

"Long enough to get you off twice," I responded, despite promising myself I wouldn't go this route with her. "Maybe three times."

A smile played on her lips. "I'll probably have to see it to believe it."

God dammit. She was hard-core flirting now, practically begging me to take her to bed, and I wanted to take her shopping instead. There was something very wrong with this picture, but I had to be strong.

"We can revisit this conversation later," I said, deflecting. "But first I have a favor to ask."

"Sure." She looked surprised but more curious than anything else.

"I only brought enough clothes for a few days and it looks like I'm going to be here a bit longer than that. Can you come shopping with me so I can pick up an extra pair of jeans and some sweats?"

"Oh, um, sure. The nearest mall is about half an hour from here, near where Connie lives. I don't go there much but they'll have everything you need."

"Would you come with me?"

"I have to get to the rink."

"Why? According to the schedule, the men's leagues play tonight, but you said the people who come to watch don't buy much, so why do you need to be there?"

She hesitated. "Well, as you've noticed, there aren't many reliable employees so I tend to hang around to make sure everything goes smoothly."

"And I appreciate that, but since you don't have to, and you certainly don't get paid enough to work that many hours, wouldn't it be more fun to hang out with me today?"

"Hmm." She pretended to be deep in thought. "*Fun.* What is this phenomenon you call fun?"

"It's really cool," I told her. "You forget about work and responsibilities, and you just hang out with someone you like for the whole day. Maybe even the night."

"Is that what last night was?" She playfully cocked her head.

I chuckled. "Last night was doing a good deed for a friend. Today is having some actual fun while hanging out."

"I suppose I could give this fun stuff a try," she deadpanned. "But I might not be very good at it."

"Don't worry." I winked. "I'm good enough for both of us."

CHAPTER TEN

Noelle

I hadn't been to the mall in a few years. I didn't have the money to shop in those brand-name stores, usually hitting secondhand places when I needed something, and I mostly stuck to the small local shops in Garland Grove. I didn't have any extra money today either, but at least I could enjoy watching Remy shop. And maybe I'd get to see him try on jeans. He was probably like most men, who bought clothes without trying them on, but it was still a fun fantasy.

We walked into Gap where he grabbed two pairs of jeans off a shelf, two pairs of sweats, and a couple of long-sleeve shirts. He didn't look at anything but the size and turned to me with a grin.

"Wanna get matching flannel?"

"What?" I blinked in confusion.

"I was thinking you'd look cute in that—" He pointed to a green and black flannel shirt on one of the racks. "And they have one for guys too. We could be twins."

I laughed. "You're almost a foot taller than me and probably a hundred pounds heavier. I'm thinking we're never going to be twins, no matter what we wear."

"Come on, let's see." He pulled the shirt in question off the rack and tossed it at me before walking back over to the men's section and grabbing a similar one. He put it on before I'd even moved and I shook my head, wondering how someone could look so hot in a flannel shirt.

"Fine." I put it on and we stood next to each other in front of one of the mirrors.

"Totally twins," he said solemnly. "I can't even tell which of us is which."

I burst out laughing. "You're kind of dorky, you know that?"

"That's a compliment, right?"

"Maybe." I tried to keep things light so he wouldn't see my inner struggle, but deep down I knew what he was doing. My clothes were old and ratty, so this was his way of buying me something new without making me feel bad.

For what felt like the hundredth time, I battled with my conscience. I wanted to spend time with him. Hell, I wanted to sleep with him. Even if I never saw him again, I wanted to know what it would be like to be intimate with him. Every fiber of my being told me it would be good, and there wasn't a whole lot of anything good in my life. It wasn't a question of morals, either, because I firmly believed a woman could enjoy sex with a man just because she wanted to. But this was different. The idea of sleeping with a man who'd just bought me clothes felt...*wrong*.

Had he noticed the holes in my socks? How old my bra was? I'd done my best to hide those things by taking them off in the dark, but he seemed to notice everything, and most of my clothes were old and worn. My jeans were ripped at the knees, I didn't own a pair of socks that didn't have at least one hole, and the soles of my winter boots were wearing thin. I had money in the bank, but that was so I could get an apartment at some point, and I'd wear everything I had until each piece fell apart before I dug into my nest egg.

If I was honest, I needed sex and companionship a hell of a lot more than I needed a new flannel shirt or socks, and Remy was the kind of man most women only ever dreamed about. He was tall and solid, with the body of a professional athlete. His shoulders filled the doorway of his room at the bed and breakfast, and the cropped dark beard on his face gave him an edgy look. His hair was such a dark brown it was almost black, which made his golden eyes stand out even more, and when he reached up to grab something from an overhead shelf, the muscles rippling in his arms made me wonder what he would look like naked.

I'd been thinking about seeing him naked a lot the last two days and was starting to feel like a teenager with a crush.

"So, what do you say? Matching flannel?" He interrupted my thoughts, and I shook my head.

"Are you trying to tell me you don't like my clothes?" I asked, taking off the flannel shirt and handing it back to him.

"Not at all. I'm telling you I want us to match."

"I live here," I said lightly. "So I'm not the one that needs clothes."

"Fine." He gave in gracefully, putting the green flannel shirts back where he'd gotten them and grabbing a black hoodie. "Okay, then, I'm done."

We walked around the mall a little while longer and I paused in front of a children's shop, staring at the display window thoughtfully.

"Do Alexander and Daphne need clothes?" he asked before I could say anything.

"Alexander does. He's growing so fast, even the pants she bought him at the beginning of the school year are starting to get a little short. I try to buy him fun things at Christmas, but this year I think I need to be more practical."

"What if—" he began.

"Don't." I turned to him, holding out a finger. "I know you're rich and can buy anything you want for anyone you want, but it's hard for regular people like me and Connie to accept gifts like that. She let you pay for the plumber because that impacted the kids—being wet and cold is dangerous, especially in the winter—but the rest of the time we manage okay."

"Do you?" He lifted one big hand and cupped the side of my face. "I like doing nice things for people. It's the holidays and I've been incredibly lucky in business. Giving back makes me happy. Why won't you let me?" His voice was filled with sincerity, and I sighed, though I couldn't back down.

"Because I've been taking care of myself since long before I met you and I'll continue to do so after you're gone. Can't we just have fun while you're here?" I leaned into the warmth of his hand because I couldn't help myself; his touch was addictive.

There was indecision in his eyes as he stared into mine, but it was shrouded in undeniable heat. The magnetism between us was hard to ignore and I unconsciously licked my lips, the need for him to kiss me almost more than I could stand. Then he tilted his head and lowered his mouth to mine. His lips were soft but more demanding than they'd been the last time he'd kissed me, his tongue slowly slipping between the seam of my lips. It was both sexy and sweet, all wrapped up like a sensual gift box of promise.

Before I had a chance to lose myself in him, it was over, and he brushed his mouth across my cheek, lips against my ear as he whispered, "This is neither the time nor the place. But we'll pick this back up later."

He slid his hand around mine and we headed for the parking garage.

"You want to get an early dinner?" he asked once we were headed back to Garland Grove.

"I'm not hungry," I said softly, squeezing his fingers.

He looked down at where our hands were linked and then stared straight ahead. "Noelle, I want to take you back to my room and lick every inch of you. I really do. But I'm leaving soon, probably for good, and I don't want you to have regrets."

"Believe it or not," I said quietly, "women are just as interested in sex as men are, and we don't all need proclamations of love to enjoy it. I'm well aware that you're leaving, and like I said earlier, I just want to enjoy the time we have together. You're not going to be here long enough for either of us to get invested, you know?"

His jaw tightened a little, but he was still staring at the road ahead so I couldn't see his eyes. That seemed to be the best way to read him, by the emotions that lurked behind those golden eyes of his, so I felt unsettled when I couldn't see them.

He was quiet for a long time before he said, "We should stop at a drugstore."

"There's one a few blocks from your bed and breakfast."

"Do they sell big boxes of condoms?"

I chuckled. "I don't know. I've never bought any there."

"I don't think those little boxes of six will be enough."

"No?"

He glanced over at me. "Probably not."

"Twelve?"

"I was thinking a supersized box of like thirty-six or something."

I laughed. "We don't have a Costco around here and I don't think I've seen a box like that at any local stores."

"Guess I'll have to stock up then."

"How long are you staying, exactly?" I asked, still chuckling.

"Probably until the twentieth or so. I'm going to Vancouver for Christmas and that's when I'm thinking of heading out."

I did a quick mental count. Today was December fourth. Which meant I had approximately sixteen more days with him. Hopefully, that would be enough.

CHAPTER ELEVEN

Remy

Sex, I thought wryly, was so much more powerful than we gave it credit for. It was biological, physical, emotional, and mental, and I couldn't think of anything else that ticked all those boxes. If you added someone you really liked to the equation, it probably hit on a bunch of other qualifiers too, and that was why I was having a tough time with this. Somewhere in the deepest recesses of my soul, I knew that if I touched her—really touched her—nothing would ever be the same.

It's only sex, I told myself as we drove to the drugstore.

You've had dozens of one-night stands, I thought as I grabbed five boxes of condoms.

"You must be Remy Knight." The woman behind the counter of the Garland Grove Apothecary had to be at least eighty, but her eyes twinkled as she rang me up.

"Yes, ma'am." I had no idea how she knew me.

"You and Noelle must have some fun plans this week," she said, putting the condoms in a bag and taking my credit card.

Christ. I'd forgotten how small towns like this could be when it came to gossip.

"You be good to her, you hear me?" The older woman didn't even look up as she ran my card. "She's had a rough time since that no-good mother of hers ran off. And Noelle's a good girl."

"Yes, ma'am. She's amazing."

She glanced up sharply. "Don't toy with her, Mr. Knight. It would make many of us here in town unhappy. Especially me."

I had no idea what to say so I just nodded and put my credit card back in my wallet. "Thank you."

"See you soon." She was smiling now, as if she hadn't just offered a veiled threat. "You two have fun!"

I practically ran back out to my rental car.

Buying condoms had probably been a bad idea.

I had no intention of hurting Noelle, but I was leaving in a little over two weeks.

She knows you're leaving, I reminded myself as I parked in my spot at the B&B.

What the hell was wrong with me? I was never this indecisive about women, but this situation was a little different and I wasn't sure how to handle it.

I kept my hand firmly wrapped around hers as we climbed the steps to my room and let ourselves in. I gave myself a little pep talk as I kept busy putting away my new clothes, leaving the bag of condoms on the floor next to the bed.

"Did I do something wrong?" Noelle asked after a few minutes of me fumbling around the room like a teenager about to get his first blow job.

"What?" I'd been so deep in my own head, the sound of her voice startled me.

"Ever since I said I was okay with casual sex, you've been quiet and...*weird*. Are you one of those guys who doesn't like it when a woman is confident in her sexuality?"

I chuckled, shaking my head as I sat next to her on the edge of the bed. "No. That's not it." I leaned over and kissed her on the cheek. "In fact, I love a woman who's confident about sex. I just don't like it when the woman is in a vulnerable situation."

"How am I vulnerable?" she asked, cocking her head slightly.

"Technically, you work for me."

"Ah." She got up and swung around, climbing up to straddle me and hooking her arms around my neck as she leaned in. "That kind of adds an element of naughty to the equation, doesn't it?"

"Fuck, Noelle." I slid my hands around so I was cupping her glorious bottom.

"Grown woman," she whispered, brushing her lips along my temple. "Grown woman who really wants to make love with you." Her hair fell forward, lightly tickling my neck and the sides of my face as she nibbled my lower lip. "Grown woman who's perfectly capable of deciding what is and isn't an acceptable risk." She ran her tongue along the soft spot behind my ear and pinpricks of heat assaulted my skin.

"You've made your point." I leaned up and captured her mouth with mine. This was probably selfish and reckless, but there was no doubt she wanted me as much as I wanted her. Her arms tightened around my neck, pulling me closer, rubbing her soft, lithe body against my chest. Her lips were pliant against mine, softening for me with each stroke of my tongue. She was beautiful, but also sensual and sexy and so damn sweet.

I took greedy pulls from her mouth, throwing caution to the wind because I was only human and she was delectable. I needed to consume her and I wasn't sure why, but I couldn't remember the last time a simple kiss had me straining against my jeans so painfully.

I slid my hands up and under the back of her T-shirt, unsnapping her bra and then lifted both the bra and shirt over her head. She was so slender in general, I'd been expecting her breasts to be small, but instead they were full and round and sat high on her chest, two beacons calling to me.

Tearing my mouth away from hers was physically painful but the need to taste her sweet blush-colored nipples was more than I could stand. I wrapped my mouth around one, lightly biting down until she started to squirm. I flicked my tongue against the hard little peak, grazing it with my teeth and then sucking it into my mouth again. I alternated kissing, licking, and sucking until she gripped the hair at the back of my neck with her fingers, her short nails digging into my scalp. Her head was thrown back, chest arched into my face, and it was all I could do to keep from throwing her down and taking her hard and rough.

Her breath was coming in short, staccato little bursts as I moved to the other breast, and she wiggled against my groin.

"Remy..." Her voice was raspy. Breathy. Filled with need.

"Are you wet for me?" I growled against her chest.

"So wet."

I finally lifted my head, gazing into her emerald eyes. I reached down to pull my Henley over my head and watched as she licked her lips.

"My turn," she whispered, dropping her head.

The warmth of her mouth on one of my nipples sent shockwaves of pleasure through my system. Women rarely paid any attention to my nipples but Noelle acted like they were her new favorite thing, sucking one into her mouth and flattening her tongue against it before moving to the other.

Damn, my chest wasn't usually an erogenous zone for me but with Noelle, my entire body reacted to her touch.

"You're beautiful," I breathed, looking down at her as she continued to worship my chest. She playfully nipped at the skin, clipping it between her teeth before going back to my nipples and running her fingers through the hair on my chest.

She slid down to the floor, settling between my legs and running her hand over the length of my erection.

"I need to taste you," she whispered.

"Fuck yeah." I managed to get my jeans and boxers off at warp speed but moved onto the bed. "Come here," I said, holding out my hand. "It'll be more comfortable for us up here."

I stretched out, watching as she shed her jeans and then joined me on the bed completely naked.

Then her mouth was on me again, but this time in a much more erotic place, and I forgot everything but her. She sucked and teased, her hand moving in tandem to her mouth, and I groaned deep in my chest.

"Jesus, Noelle…damn, baby, just like that." I was starting to move in and out of her mouth, guiding the rhythm as she opened her mouth wider to take all of me.

This time I was the one digging my fingers in her hair, fisting the bulk of it but letting her stay in control. I was embarrassingly close and when my cock hit the back of her throat, I lost any and all semblance of power because it was all-encompassing. I shot off into her mouth hard and fast, holding her head until I was done because it was so fucking hot to watch.

"Goddamn." I reached down and pulled her on top of me, letting her curl into my shoulder. "That was incredible."

"I love doing that," she said with what sounded like a happy sigh. "Being responsible for bringing you that kind of pleasure totally gets me off."

"Give me five minutes and you'll be getting off a few more times."

She moved up to find my mouth again and the moment our lips touched we were off and running again. My erection was still at half-mast, gearing up to go full throttle for the second time. I was good to go three or four times in a night, but it usually took more than two minutes to get there.

"Condoms," I murmured as she straddled me.

She leaned over the bed, grabbing the bag they were in, and hurriedly opened one of the boxes, pulling out a handful. She opened a package, took out the condom, and then leaned down to suck me deep again.

I groaned, shuddering against the exquisite torture of having her mouth on me again so soon after getting off, but it had the desired effect because I was hard as stone and ready to go.

"Noelle." Her name sounded strange on my lips, but when her eyes met mine without stopping what she was doing, I almost lost it all over again.

She moved her mouth but kept her hand on the base of my shaft as she rolled the condom on. It had been a long time since a woman put a condom on me, but it was so hot, I had to grab the sheet beneath my hands to keep from dragging her up and sitting her right where I wanted her. Luckily, I didn't have to wait long because she crawled over me and positioned herself over my groin, inching down a tiny bit at a time and letting me fill her.

We groaned in unison as she sank all the way down, her hands on my shoulders as she leaned forward. We just stared at one another, our gazes so completely focused on each other that neither of us moved. I wanted Noelle to have her way. She'd been in control since the beginning, so there was no reason for me to change anything unless she asked me to. A woman in control was sexy *as fuck*, and Noelle put other women to shame when she fixed her eyes on mine.

"You feel so good," she murmured, clenching around me.

"You're so tight and wet," I whispered back, my hands making small swirls on her hips. "Ride me, beautiful."

She started to move, and while I would normally take over and start thrusting up and in, I didn't. Her hips had begun to gyrate, and she took her time, moving up and down slowly. She'd ease out to the tip and then slide down painstakingly slowly, as if we had all the time in the world. And I suppose we did. There was nowhere I had to be, and no work that couldn't wait until morning, which meant we could stay in this bed all night. Doing whatever we wanted.

I reached up, closing my hands over her breasts and gently rubbing my thumbs over her nipples. They were so responsive, immediately hardening at my touch, and her eyes slowly closed. She was moving a little faster now, fingers digging into my shoulders as she bit her lower lip.

"That's right, baby. Show me when I hit the spot." I pressed deeper into her, angling my hips a little to go further. I did it a few times, testing out which angles she liked best, but I was already spinning from arousal, fighting to keep my second orgasm at bay. She hadn't come yet tonight and for me to get off twice before she did was unheard of.

"Remy...more." She was rocking back and forth, her breath coming in little gasps, and I took her cue that it was time to take over.

"Look at me, beautiful." I wanted her gorgeous green eyes trained on me when she came.

"Remy!" Her orgasm caught us both off guard because she gasped just as I felt her jerk and tighten around me. Her fingers dug into the flesh of my shoulders as she cried out, and I was right behind her.

"Oh wow." She collapsed on my chest, her hair draping across one of my arms. "That was...wonderful. Really, really incredible."

"It was," I agreed.

"Can we do it again?"

Woman after my own heart.

CHAPTER TWELVE

Noelle

It had been a while since I'd had an all-night sex fest, so when I got up in the morning, my nether regions tingled from the exertion. Remy was everything I'd imagined he'd be in bed—and more. So much so that I hadn't been able to get enough. His staying power was impressive, and the moment we touched, he was ready to go. In the light of day, though, I felt an uncomfortable urge to get going. It would be so easy to just lose myself in him, but that wasn't an option. I was an adult, but small-town living meant everyone knew everything and Rudy was undoubtedly on the phone telling half the town I'd spent two nights with Remy Knight.

"Where are you off to?" Remy asked as I got dressed after my shower.

"Need to get to the arena and check the ice machine—it probably needs a good cleaning. Then I have some errands to run."

"You don't have to go," he said quietly, his eyes finding mine. "I'd like you to stay."

I smiled. "I'd like that too, but I have to be careful. This is a small town and everyone I've ever known is probably going to know I'm sleeping with the infamous Remington Knight. It's better I don't give them anything else to talk about."

He sighed. "I'm sorry. I didn't even think about that, but I should have."

"It's all right."

"I booked a hotel room in Vancouver for the night of the game. Is that okay?"

"Of course. Much better than driving home late at night, especially this time of year when you never know what the weather will be."

Not that either of us were thinking about driving home. Based on the way he was looking at me, he was contemplating all the fun we could have in a hotel room far away from the nosy neighbors here in Garland Grove. Which was exactly what I was thinking about.

"We could leave tomorrow morning," he said, grabbing his keys as we got ready to go. "Spend the day in Vancouver, have an early dinner, and then go to the game."

"I like to be there for the warm-ups," I told him. "Is that okay?"

"Sure. You want to go down to ice level?"

"Of course. That's half the fun!" I laughed, grabbing my bag.

We walked out to his rental and he opened the door for me. I climbed up and settled against the comfortable leather seats. I was already getting spoiled, riding around in an SUV with all the bells and whistles, sleeping in a warm, comfortable bed, and getting taken out to nice dinners. Sleeping at the arena tonight was going to suck, but at least I had tomorrow night to look forward to.

"What are you going to do today?" I asked him as he headed for the arena.

"I'm going to spend the day on the phone, taking care of all the things I've let slide since I got here."

"Owning a hockey team must be pretty cool," I said softly. "I'll be excited to watch them on TV. I bet you'll be a nervous wreck opening night."

"Probably."

"Were you nervous when you played? Like right before a game?"

"Not nervous, so much as anxious, like ready to go. That last fifteen minutes between when we were dressed and warmed up, and when the game actually started, used to drive me nuts. I could never sit still."

"Sounds like it."

"What about you? Were you nervous before you played?"

"Always," I said, chuckling. "But the minute my feet hit the ice, I forgot everything but the game."

"Me too." He glanced at me and we smiled, a warmth passing between us that hadn't been there before. Last night had been so, so good. Absolutely the best sex I'd ever had, and I was struggling to be casual about it in the aftermath. I'd had good sex before, but it hadn't felt like this, and I didn't understand why. Remy wasn't like other men, though, and certainly not like anyone I'd ever dated. He was the whole package—the kind of man women fell head over heels for.

And I didn't have that option.

He'd be gone in two weeks and I'd still be here, working and trying to figure out when I could afford an apartment. Even a studio. All I needed was a warm bed, a bathroom, somewhere to keep my stuff, and a microwave. I'd pawned or sold most of my stuff, including my TV and a good portion of my household stuff. For one thing, I'd needed the money. For another, I had nowhere to keep it all.

Six months, I told myself firmly. If I kept on doing what I was doing for six more months, I'd have enough to get a small place to live. And if Remy came through on getting me a raise, I'd be able to breathe for the first time in a long time.

"Whatcha thinkin' about?" he asked as we pulled up to the arena.

"Nothing in particular." I grabbed my bag out of the back. "So I guess I'll see you tomorrow?"

"Hey." He got out of the car and came around to my side.

"Hmm?" I looked up to find him lowering his mouth to mine, his lips gentle but strangely possessive. They caressed mine as if he owned them—and me—and I inadvertently sighed.

"You sure you don't want to sleep over tonight?" he murmured, his mouth hovering a fraction of an inch from mine.

"I do, but it's better if we don't." I quickly kissed him one last time and turned to go, but his arms tightened around me, keeping me tight against his solid chest.

"Last night was awesome, Noelle." His knuckles grazed my cheek.

"It was."

"I'm looking forward to spending tomorrow with you."

"Me too." I reluctantly took a step back, smiled, and hurried into the arena without looking back. A little distance would be good for us.

Well, for me anyway.

I absolutely could not get hooked on this guy.

No way, no how.

———

We left at eight the next morning, heading to Vancouver. I'd gone to university there and though Garland Grove was home, I'd loved my time living there. I'd had a scholarship that covered almost everything, so it had been the only four years of my life I hadn't been worried about money. I had a place to live, food, and I loved school. Those had been good years and coming to Vancouver reminded me of them.

It was a nice day walking around, even though it was cold, but I'd worn two long-sleeve T-shirts beneath my hoodie and remembered my gloves this time. And with Remy's arm around me as often as possible, I wasn't even thinking about being cold. He was nothing like what I'd imagined a professional athlete, even a retired one, would be like. He was a big guy, but gentle and sweet, always opening doors, pulling out chairs, and offering to buy me things. He seemed to take my refusals in stride, but kept trying, which was as endearing as it was infuriating.

"I have a gift for you tonight," he said as we walked up to the arena where the Vipers played. "It's already bought and paid for, and the money went to charity, so please don't say no."

I arched my brows as he collected our tickets at will call and a Vancouver Vipers-themed shopping bag. He turned and handed it to me. "What is it?" I asked in confusion.

"Open it."

I opened the bag and gasped, slowly pulling out a jersey that appeared to have been autographed by the whole team.

"If it makes you feel any better, I didn't pay the team for it," he said. "I made a donation to the team's charity of choice, and they did this for me. Which I did for you."

"Remy." Tears puddled in my eyes because there was zero chance I was going to refuse this gift. I loved the Vipers and had never been able to afford a jersey. To have it signed by the whole team was incredibly thoughtful and I threw my arms around his neck. "Thank you."

"Don't cry." He wrapped his strong arms around me. "Do you like it?"

"No." I shook my head. "I love it."

"Good." He stroked my cheek. "Put it on."

I yanked off my hoodie and pulled the jersey over my head, looking down in excitement. "This is amazing."

"Look at the rest of what's in the bag."

I dug through the contents and found a travel coffee mug, team socks, a team calendar, and a commemorative puck, also signed by someone, but I didn't recognize the signature.

"This is too much," I whispered. "Why would they do this?"

"Because I made a huge donation and asked them to," he said, pulling me up against him again. "I wanted tonight to be memorable."

"Every night with you is memorable."

Our eyes met and he kissed me. Right there on the concourse, like no one else in the world existed, his hands circling my waist. I wrapped one arm around his neck since the other was holding the shopping bag, and I kissed him back like he was mine. Like this was more than just a short-term distraction in my very mundane life.

"I don't know where you learned to kiss," I whispered against his mouth, "but you could probably open a school or something and women everywhere would thank you."

He chuckled. "My hands are pretty full these days, but we can talk about it." He looped his arm around my shoulders and we headed toward our seats.

"Mr. Knight! Mr. Knight!" A young woman who didn't look a day over twenty came running over to us. "I'm Beth Bennett with the Vipers. Mr. Tiffoli, the team owner, would love it if you joined him in his box tonight." She was out of breath, as if she'd run to find us, and Remy glanced at me.

"Do you want to? I have pretty awesome seats."

"It's up to you," I said softly.

"Mr. Tiffoli said he very much wanted to meet you." Beth seemed a little anxious and I squeezed Remy's hand.

I hated that our indecision was stressing her out. "It's fine," I told Remy. "We can go up to the box for a while and then go to our seats."

Remy nodded and laced his fingers through mine as we followed Beth to a private elevator. We went up a few levels and exited on the concourse where the suites and private boxes were located.

"I'm probably going to have to talk shop for a while," he whispered against my ear. "But I'll try to keep it short."

"It's fine. I love hockey and once the game starts, I won't even remember who you are." I laughed and he shook his head, grinning back at me.

God, he was hot.

"Remington Knight!" A short man with a shock of white hair and a loud, booming voice addressed us the moment we stepped inside the box and Remy immediately extended his hand.

"Mr. Tiffoli."

Introductions were made, someone put a plate of food in my hand, and as he'd predicted, Remy was swept away with business talk. He glanced over at me a few times, but I waved him off, happy to sip a glass of chardonnay, nibble on appetizers even though we'd already eaten, and look down at the ice. Warm-ups had started and we were up here instead of down there, but it was okay. Remy had already made this game special, so I didn't mind missing out. Especially since our regular seats were behind the home bench.

Despite what I'd told him, there was nothing that would make me forget Remington Knight. Not hockey, not the warm-ups, not even sitting behind the bench. Tonight had been epic so far, but it was far more about the man than the gifts or VIP treatment. Autographed jerseys and awesome seats were fun; Remy, on the other hand, was special. I'd stopped believing in happily-ever-after a long time ago, but if there was such a thing, the only man I could imagine it with was him.

CHAPTER THIRTEEN

Remy

Noelle loved hockey. I'd figured she was a fan, but I hadn't expected to hear her chirping at the players, whistling louder than anyone else in the arena, or following every move like she'd written the team's playbook. The Vipers were down 2–1 by the middle of the second period, and now that we were in our seats behind the bench, she was lit up and fully engaged. She was totally focused on what was happening on the ice.

"Seriously, Thomson?" she muttered when one of the rookies turned over the puck and Calgary almost got another goal against the Vipers.

"He's young," I said. "Still learning."

"He's a professional hockey player making...how much do rookie players make? Almost a million? Yeah, for a million dollars, he shouldn't be making those kinds of mistakes." She shook her head.

I chuckled. "Uh huh. Easy to say from here in the stands. Get out there in front of twenty thousand screaming fans and—"

"One. Million. Dollars." She wiggled a finger in my face. "Give me a million dollars and I'll make a lot less mistakes than Thomson has made tonight."

"I'm not letting you near my rookies when I get to Fort Lauderdale," I deadpanned.

She laughed. "Let me at them—I'll whip them into shape."

Somehow, I believed her and the idea of having her with me in Fort Lauderdale was interesting.

She turned back to the game, watching as Calgary stole the puck and skated toward Vancouver's net. Vancouver's captain glided after him, but with no real speed or hustle.

"Come on!" Noelle yelled, getting to her feet. "Are you gonna back-check at some point tonight or what?!"

I snorted out a laugh. She was hilarious, but obviously knew the game almost as well as I did. Her comments mirrored my thoughts, but as a former player, I understood the nuances of playing in front of hard-core crowds like this one, which was probably the only piece of the puzzle missing for her.

"Oh, geez, there's Thomson again," she sighed. "I don't think this is going to end well."

"How about a little encouragement for the kid?" I countered. "He's barely shaving, making almost a million dollars a year, and his job is in front of zillions of fans all over the world. Poor kid probably hasn't even had his dick sucked yet."

She turned to me, her eyes wide, and we both burst out laughing. "I'm going to bet he's getting laid on the regular, but you're right, I should probably cut him some slack. I forget he's only eighteen. It just seems to me that if you're good enough to make the starting lineup at eighteen, you shouldn't make dumb mistakes."

"We all make mistakes, even after a decade, while earning ten million. For one thing, we're all human, but for another, this is a high-profile, high-stress job. Yeah, we make a lot of money, but we earn every penny. The sacrifices in your personal life, the physical impact even without injuries, and the mental stress. Hearing people heckling you every time you're in a different arena is hard, but hearing your own fans yelling insults? That sucks. You get used to it, and we all learn to deal with it, but it's never fun."

"Okay, fine. I'll yell at Calgary's players then—that's right, Hovisk, go sit in the box and think about what you did!"

Noelle was definitely an equal opportunity chirper.

Vancouver pulled out a win in overtime and Noelle talked about the game nonstop on the way to the hotel. I loved seeing her so excited, her eyes glittering as she talked about the game-winning goal and how the team had battled back. I'd never dated a woman who loved hockey as much as I did, and it was fun seeing it from the perspective of a fan who wasn't gushing over my skills or history on the ice. In fact, my life as a hockey player had never come up other than when she'd asked if I got nervous before games, and that was yet another thing I liked about her.

If I was honest, I liked everything about her, and even though emails and texts that needed my attention were piling up, I wasn't focused on anything but the beautiful blond who'd just undressed for me.

I unbuttoned my shirt and let it fall off my shoulders, noting how she watched me, her eyes moving down my torso hungrily.

"At first it was your eyes," she murmured, crawling onto the bed and leaning back against the pillows. "So golden and soulful, as if you can see right through me."

She ran her hands over her breasts, squeezing them lightly. "Then it was that damn V," she continued, focusing on my abdomen. "Because what woman doesn't love the V?"

She spread her legs and bent her knees, one hand traveling to the apex between her legs. "But now I'm pretty sure it's just you. Because watching you stand there in your jeans has me so wet, I'm about to start without you." Her eyes met mine and she slowly licked her lips.

I pulled off my jeans and boxers in two seconds flat, before sliding onto the bed and positioning myself between her legs.

"Do I get to watch?" I asked in a low voice.

"Sure." She touched herself with gentle precision but the temptation was too much for me. Watching was fun but participating was better, and before I could help myself, I moved her hand away and replaced it with my mouth. Her hips came up off the bed and she moaned, her legs shaking as I pulled her knees over my shoulders.

I took my time, using my tongue, lips, and hands to explore every inch of her. I'd been inside of her several times already, but we hadn't done this yet. She was all woman too, soft and warm and wet, with a musky scent and a sweet, tangy flavor. When I pushed a finger inside of her, she clenched around me, her thighs tightening on the sides of my head.

"You taste like heaven," I whispered, diving back in for more.

"Then someone should kill me," she panted.

I chuckled, suckling the tender skin of her folds, using the tip of my tongue to tease her. I circled her clit until she was whimpering with need, her body covered in a light sheen of sweat and her voice getting raspier each time she cried out.

"More?" I asked, lifting my head to look at her.

"God, yes!"

I pushed my tongue inside of her and pinched her clit with my thumb and forefinger. Her shriek bounced off the walls as she came, her body erupting in pleasure as she bucked against me.

It was fucking beautiful too.

Watching a woman come was always one of my favorite things about sex; watching Noelle come was one of my favorite things in life. I'd never known how much I enjoyed it until now because I didn't even care about getting myself off. Pleasing her was the only thing on my mind, and I'd give up my own orgasms to watch her have more. Luckily, I didn't have to, but in that moment I would have.

"I hope you brought a lot of condoms," she said, reaching for me.

I covered her body with mine and kissed her. "Two whole boxes."

———

I was up early and let Noelle sleep as I pulled out my laptop, signed in with the hotel's Wi-Fi and checked emails. I really needed to be in Fort Lauderdale, but with Christmas so close and my family in Vancouver, I'd made the decision to stay. I'd be in Garland Grove until the twentieth and head to Florida on the twenty-sixth.

Well, that was the plan, but as I gazed over at the beautiful woman sleeping beside me, I realized I didn't want to leave her. Not when everything was going so well and we were having so much fun. I didn't have time for a relationship, but after a week with her, I wanted her more than I'd wanted a woman in ages. Maybe ever. The problem was that I had to leave and she had to stay.

Or did she?

I looked over at her and contemplated asking her to come to Fort Lauderdale with me for a while. She didn't like me giving her money or buying her things, but I was willing to bet she'd never taken a paid vacation from the rink, and I could make that happen. According to the accountant I'd hired, the books were a mess. Taxes and bills were paid, but beyond that, there was no one in charge, no one keeping an eye on things on a day-to-day basis, and no rhyme or reason to the way things operated. I'd been considering offering Noelle the job of manager of the whole arena, but if I did that, how could she come visit me regularly in Florida?

It was way too soon to be thinking about a relationship, but there was no reason we couldn't continue what we'd started once I headed to Florida. I could afford to fly her back and forth, and maybe if things were still going well, we could reassess in a few months.

"Are you working?" she murmured sleepily, her face still half buried in the pillow.

"Did I wake you?" I asked, putting a hand on her bare shoulder. "I'm sorry."

"It's okay." She turned over and stretched, giving me an unimpeded view of her beautiful breasts. "What time are we heading back to Garland Grove?"

"Whenever we feel like it. I was going to work for a while and then order breakfast. We don't have to check out until noon."

"I could eat," she said, smiling lazily, her eyes fluttering closed again.

"You look like you could sleep longer," I said.

"I could, but I like it better when you're under the covers with me instead of sitting up working."

Suddenly, work didn't seem that important. I closed my laptop, put it on the floor next to the bed, and slid beneath the covers, pulling her against my chest.

"Like this?"

"Mmhm." She nestled against me and within a few minutes her breathing evened out and I knew she was asleep.

I watched her for a little while, but I must have drifted off too, because the next time I opened my eyes it was after ten and I heard her in the bathroom. I ordered breakfast and then joined her in the shower. We made love, ate, packed up our things, and got back on the road, even though I would have liked to stay in Vancouver longer. I'd already started to crave having her beside me at night, and I didn't want to go back to the bed and breakfast where she felt uncomfortable staying with me.

There was no help for it, though, because everything else in Garland Grove was sold out. I'd called around after she'd told me people might talk about her spending nights with me, but every place I'd found with a little more privacy was fully booked so there hadn't been much choice. I already knew she wouldn't take more than another day or so off work, especially with some big event happening tomorrow night at the rink.

"Hey, what time does the thing at the arena start tomorrow?" I asked her as I drove.

"Six," she said.

"Are you going to be outside the whole time?"

"I'll probably be in and out, but for the most part, yes. Dwayne will be keeping up with making popcorn as needed and hopefully two big urns of hot chocolate will be enough."

"Do you do it every year?"

"Yeah. We unofficially consider it the official kickoff for the holiday season, even though that's not really accurate since the tree in the center of town technically is, but no one cares. It's a big, fun night of skating, Christmas music, and hot chocolate, and we're usually packed. It's only five dollars to get in, which includes skate rental, so even though it's not a moneymaker, it's a goodwill kind of thing."

I nodded. "Sounds like fun. Have you always done it?"

"I came up with the idea my first holiday season working there and then it stuck."

"And you run it?"

"For the most part."

"Thank you for taking care of my arena when apparently no one else has." I reached for her hand.

"Thank you for noticing."

"I notice everything about you, Noelle."

CHAPTER FOURTEEN

Noelle

I knew he meant it as a compliment, but his words made me feel a little weird. He obviously didn't notice *everything* or he would have figured out I was homeless by now, and while I didn't want him to know, I also didn't like keeping such a big secret from him based on our rapidly growing intimacy. It was just so freakin' embarrassing, and he was so damn successful, I couldn't imagine admitting that I'd lost everything and was in the process of starting over. I was almost there—six more months—but in the meantime, it was humiliating.

It was also ironic. The people of Garland Grove were generally kind and caring, while simultaneously spectacularly nosy. Sleeping with Remy Knight? It was undoubtedly the main topic of conversation at the diner on Main Street, but Noelle Burrier living out of her car? No one had picked up on it other than Dwayne. So hiding it from Remy was almost second nature, despite the fact that I longed to tell him. I wanted to curl up in his arms and explain, bask in his warmth and strength, and let him know I was almost there.

I must have sighed out loud because he glanced over at me. "Did I say something wrong?" he asked.

"No." I shook my head. "I'm a little sad we had to leave Vancouver. That's all."

"You want to go back?" he asked. "I can talk to my assistant and check email from anywhere."

"We can't. I have to check in at the arena and make sure the coffee urns are working since I haven't used them in months."

"How about I come to work with you and then we can go out? You want to catch a movie or something?"

I hesitated. How many times could we go out without him asking to go to my place? What would I say? How could I explain that I didn't live anywhere right now? The only way to avoid that would be to either go back to the bed and breakfast with him, or not see him at all. I could say I had plans with friends, but I didn't want to. God knows, I wanted to spend every waking moment with him. Hell, I wanted to spend all moments with him, waking or not.

"Seems like a long time to think about whether or not you want to go to a movie," he said after a moment.

"I'm not used to...dating," I said finally. "And frankly, we're back to the same situation, where everyone is going to see us together and then I'm going to be the small-town girl the billionaire hockey star hooked up with while he was in town, before heading off into the sunset."

His fingers threaded through mine and this time he sighed. "I fucking hate that. Not just that people in small towns are nosy, but also that you think I'm just going to head off like that."

"Aren't you?"

"Well, I'm definitely leaving to go to Florida, but there's no reason you can't come visit or that we can't keep seeing each other. I don't know where, if anywhere, this is going, but I have no plans to ride off into the sunset or some such nonsense. I like you, Noelle."

I swallowed down an uncomfortable lump in my throat. "I, uh, haven't had a lot of luck with people sticking around in my life. One way or another, they all disappear."

"That's not me, babe. That's not what real men do."

I chuckled but there was no humor in it. "Yeah, well, starting with my dad, that's not been my experience."

"Every day brings the potential for new experiences—and that's what we have with us."

I nodded, though I wasn't sure I believed him. "You're sweet," was all I said.

"I'm sweet on you." He lifted our linked hands and pressed a soft kiss on the inside of my wrist.

"You won't be saying that when I put you to work this afternoon," I quipped, trying to lighten the mood because I didn't know how to talk to a guy who seemed to really like me. When was the last time I'd been out with a guy I liked as much as he liked me?

"The harder you work me, the quicker we can be done and I can take you home and ravage you. You want to go to your—"

Nope. Not going there. I interrupted him before he could finish that thought. "I think if we stay out late and sneak in after Rudy is asleep, he might not notice."

"I don't like the idea of people gossiping about you," he said firmly. "I mean, I don't give a shit what anyone thinks of me, but I won't do anything that could hurt you long-term."

I shrugged. "Long-term I'll be fine. Short-term is the problem."

"Short-term, I'm right here." He kept our hands in his lap even though it forced me to scoot over as far as I could in the passenger seat. "Also, just FYI, I'm not a billionaire. Multi-millionaire, yes, but not a billionaire."

For some reason, that made me smile.

After a few hours cleaning and fighting with the two big coffee urns I planned to use to keep the hot chocolate warm, I made sure there was enough popcorn and then we called it a day. I desperately needed clean clothes, especially if I was going to stay with him tonight, but how did I explain the fact that they were in my car? I was starting to hate the secrets I was keeping, and it was on the tip of my tongue to just tell him everything.

"I should move my car," I told him as we walked out to the parking lot. "I might as well drive over to the bed and breakfast with you so I can take off in the morning without making you drive me. I have a few things to do before the skating party and I know you have to keep up with work."

"You sure you want to park there?" he asked, pulling me against him.

"I'm suddenly tired of sneaking around like I'm a teenager breaking curfew. I'm an adult and even though there'll be some gossip, I'm sure, it's nothing I can't handle. And to be honest, I like sneaking around with you." I wound my arms around his neck. "I like being with you. And I'm not going to let a bunch of busybodies ruin it for me."

"That's the best news I've heard all week." He pressed his lips to mine. "All right, do you want to park your car there now and then we can go to the movies or should we come back later and get it?"

"Let's do it now. Rudy knows me so he'll recognize my car. If he's going to gossip, I can't stop him." I was so tired of lying, this just made it a little easier. If my reputation took a hit, I could handle it. And if

Remy was serious that we might see each other again, that would shut everyone up. At least that's what I was telling myself.

"Okay." He kissed my forehead and got into his rental while I fired up the RAV4. I'd let him drive off and then grab some clean clothes out of the hamper in the back before following him. I hadn't been sleeping at the arena enough to get my laundry done, so I was going to have to take care of that sooner rather than later, but it was going to be tricky. Why was everything in my life so complicated?

I should have been used to it by now, but I wasn't. I wasn't used to being homeless and I'd never get used to being so completely alone. With Remy in my life, I suddenly didn't feel that way anymore and it was nice.

Hell, it was more than nice.

It was awesome.

The Holiday Appreciation Skate at the rink was always a blast, and even though it was a lot of work for me, I enjoyed running it and being part of it. We'd decorated the outdoor rink and since there was an hour before the doors opened, I'd dug out the box of my personal Christmas decorations and started putting them up in the lounge. My grandmother's old lighted ceramic tree was on the coffee table in front of the fireplace, tinsel on the mantle, and I'd used some garland to hang ornaments on a few lamps. It wasn't much, but better than nothing.

I'd sold my four-foot artificial tree last December because it had been the only way to have enough money to buy some things for Alexander. I'd been sad about it, but I didn't have room for it in the car anyway, and Alexander was growing so fast he'd needed the new winter coat more than I needed an old Christmas tree I didn't even have anywhere to put up.

"Hey, what's all this?" Remy came into the lounge looking about as hot as a guy in jeans and a sweater could be. His broad shoulders seemed to fill the room and I already knew how great his ass looked in jeans.

"A little decorating. I use my own stuff since my current living situation isn't conducive to holiday decorations," I said carefully. "It makes me feel good to see my stuff here since this is where I spend most of my time anyway."

"We should go shopping for stuff just for the rink," he said, looking around. He walked over to the coffee table, pointing at the ceramic tree. "You know this is an antique, right? My grandmother had one.

They're worth money. You shouldn't leave it here where someone could break it."

I hadn't realized it was an antique. "I didn't know that. It's literally the only thing I have from my mom's mom."

"Let's pack it back up and tomorrow we can go shopping for decorations for the whole arena and you can keep your personal stuff safe. It'll be fun to decorate anyway, don't you think?"

I smiled. "Okay." I got out the box and started putting the ceramic tree away again. I felt him behind me, one big, warm hand on my back as I put the tree away. Then I turned and moved against him, letting him kiss me.

"Get a room, for Christ's sake." A deep male voice made us jump apart and I smiled at one of the hockey league coaches, Jacques "Jock" Frontier.

He was a nice guy, despite his ribbing. "Hey, Jock. Have you met Remy Knight, the new owner of the arena? Remy, Jock coaches the fourteen- and fifteen-year-old team."

The two men eyed each other before Remy approached him, holding out his hand.

"Hey, Jock." The two men shook hands.

"So it's true." Jacques cocked his head. "You're the owner now? I'd heard rumors but wasn't sure it was accurate."

"I am. I had no idea my dad even owned the place." Remy looked around with a faint smile. "So no one was more surprised than I was."

"And now you're gonna sell it." Jacques looked a little annoyed, and that was saying something since he was a pretty quiet guy who kept to himself when he wasn't coaching.

"I haven't made any decisions yet," Remy replied patiently. "I'm trying to get a feel for the place, see what's what before I do anything."

"How do you two know each other?" I asked curiously.

"We played together a long time ago," Remy said.

"Hey, Noelle, where do you want the coffee urns?" Dwayne stuck his head in the door.

"Oh, let me show you. Excuse me, guys." I headed after Dwayne but glanced over my shoulder at Jacques and Remy. It had never occurred to me they might have played together even though I knew Jacques was a retired player. Hopefully, they'd been friends.

CHAPTER FIFTEEN

Remy

Jacques and I had played together one season early in my career. He'd been older, married, and a goalie, so our paths hadn't crossed much outside the rink, but he'd been a nice enough guy. I'd had no idea he'd wound up here in Garland Grove, but there was no opportunity to ask.

"What are you really doing here?" Jacques asked me, squinting slightly. "You didn't need to come all the way out to BC just to sell the place."

I was surprised by his directness, but I liked direct, and I had nothing to hide about my intentions. "I came because I grew up skating here in the winter. I figured I'd just see the place one more time and then, somehow, I got sucked into the day-to-day activities."

"You got sucked into the activities or you got sucked into Noelle?"

I scowled. "That's none of your business."

"Maybe not, but she's a nice girl, and—"

"Woman." I gave him a look. "She's a grown woman."

"Fine. She's a nice *woman*, and guys like you…" He met my gaze and arched his brows a little.

"Guys like me?" I cocked my head questioningly. If he had something to say, he needed to say it.

"Come on, we both know the life."

"We're both out of the life, though. Retired and moving on to other things."

It seemed like he wanted to say more, but I figured his hesitation was a good time to change the subject, because anything that had to do with my relationship with Noelle was off-limits. "So, does your team have a game tonight?"

He shook his head. "I brought my younger kids to the holiday thing. They enjoyed it last year."

"How many you got? Three?"

He chuckled. "Five."

I gaped. "Five? Jesus, you're a better man than I am."

Jacques shrugged as a kid of about eight or nine came bounding into the room. "Daddy, are we going skating now? Are we?"

"Comin', buddy." He turned to go. "Good to see you, Remy. Take care. And do me a favor—let me know what you decide to do about the rink. I'd hate to see some investor buy it for the land and tear it down to build condos."

I hadn't thought of that and mentally grimaced, but nodded as I said, "I will. Take care."

Now I had another problem to consider. I definitely didn't want the rink destroyed and replaced with a strip mall or something.

Shit.

There was a line out the door as people lined up to rent skates and buy tickets. It was only five dollars to get in and that included skate rental, popcorn, and hot chocolate. There were bleachers that ran along one side of the outdoor rink, and they slowly filled with parents and teenagers who were either watching their kids skate or huddling up for warmth since it was cold as balls tonight. Dwayne was handling skate rentals while Tandy took everyone's money and Noelle was outside doling out refreshments.

She was a force of nature too, serving hot chocolate and popcorn without missing a beat. The wind had picked up once the sun went down and I frowned as I realized she wasn't wearing a coat or gloves. Had I ever seen her in a coat? She usually wore several shirts and then a hoodie.

This was so frustrating to me because despite our deepening intimacy, she had secrets. I had no doubt about that, but it confused me because she had to know she could trust me by now. Didn't she? It had only been a week, but damn, we were about as close as two people could be. Sure, it took time to truly trust someone, and I understood that too, but the fact that I'd never seen her in a winter coat bothered me. I had to tread carefully, though.

In my heart of hearts, I figured she was embarrassed. She rarely went home—wherever that was—and everything she owned was old or well-worn. From her car, that had to be more than a decade old, to her clothes, to the fatigue in her eyes. I loved watching her sleep because it seemed she didn't do that nearly enough.

My phone buzzed in my pocket and I pulled it out curiously.

Trevor Gaines was the General Manager of the Knights, someone I'd hired last summer, and we kept in touch almost daily. We hadn't talked much since I'd been in Garland Grove, but that was probably why he was calling. Except it was six-thirty in the evening here, which made it nine-thirty on the east coast, and that worried me enough to answer even though I hadn't planned to.

"Hey, what's up?" I asked.

"Sorry to bother you after business hours, but we need to talk before tomorrow and this is the first chance I've had to breathe today."

"I'm sorry I've left you to handle everything," I replied. "I've gotten a little caught up in this damn rink I inherited here in BC, but talk to me. What's going on?" I walked back inside the arena, where it would be a little quieter.

"We've had two virtual interviews with Anatoli Petrov for the head coaching position, but we need a face-to-face. He has availability this week and the beginning of next, but after that he said he's out until the start of the new year—family obligations."

"Shit. I guess I could fly to Florida for a day, do the interview, and come right back." I said, mostly to myself though I said it out loud.

"Remy, what's going on with you and this rink? I thought you were going to go, hire a realtor, and get the hell out? We have a ton of shit going on, and while I'm happy to carry a bit of the load, we're heading into the holidays and come January second, you're going to need to be here."

"I'll be there by then, but it's almost Christmas and my mom is in Vancouver, which is nearby, so I decided to stay. It also came to my attention that real estate investors might be interested in the land the rink is on, and that's a big no. The people in this town need this rink. Not only do people work here, but there are also dozens of kids and men's leagues, and no other rink for at least an hour. I'm not going to let a buyer tear it down."

He grunted. "I get that, but opening night for the Knights is liter-ally in ten months. After losing Reggie, we need a new head coach sewn up by the new year."

Our original choice for a head coach, Reggie Banks, had a heart attack last month, and after surgery had said he couldn't commit to the job. So we'd had to scramble to start the hiring process again, and a former player named Anatoli Petrov had thrown his hat in the ring. Toli had been an amazing player, someone I'd played with for two seasons, so I knew firsthand what a stellar human being he was. I'd reached out to him first, but he'd originally said he wasn't in a position to move his young family. I hadn't had a chance to talk to him since he'd started interviewing with my staff, but I figured I should call him.

"Let me give him a call," I said at last. "And I'll get back to you."

"All right. I'd really like this sewn up before year-end."

"Got it. I'll be in touch." I disconnected and went back outside. Noelle's line had slowed down now that most people were skating and I suddenly got an idea. I went back in and headed to the skate rental booth, leaning on the counter.

"Dwayne, do you know what size skate Noelle wears?" I asked him.

"An eight," he replied, grinning.

"You got a pair for her? I'm going to make her take a break and skate with me."

He nodded, reaching under the counter and producing a pair of skates. "Here you go."

"Thanks."

I headed back to the outdoor rink and sank down on the bench next to Noelle, holding out the skates. "Put these on."

She looked down in surprise. "I can't. I have to—"

"There's no line, everyone is skating, and you deserve a break. We'll be able to see if people are lining up for hot chocolate."

She gazed up at me for a second and then flashed me a little grin. "Okay." She took off her sneakers and laced up her skates while I put on my own. I got up and held out my hand to her. She took it and we stepped onto the ice.

I couldn't remember a time I'd ever skated with a girlfriend.

Noelle wasn't technically my girlfriend, but we were involved, and skating together was nice. Actually, it was more than nice. I didn't get on the ice very often these days, getting my workouts in at a gym, but I missed it. Having Noelle at my side made it that much better, and she had a big smile on her face.

"I didn't realize how much I'd missed skating," she said, all but reading my mind as her fingers twined with mine.

"Me either," I admitted. "I've convinced myself I don't miss hockey as much as I did when I first had to retire, but it's a lie. I miss it every fucking day."

"I'm sorry, babe." She moved closer to me, squeezing my hand. "Is it too late to try again? Even just one season?"

I smiled down at her, though her words were like a punch to the throat. "My doctors all said it was too dangerous. My heart is in good shape now, after the surgery, but the kind of strain athletes put on their hearts makes it riskier than we'd like. I'd literally be chancing another heart attack."

She grimaced. "Then I'm glad you're not playing because I wouldn't want to lose you."

"You don't have to worry about it. That ship has sailed."

"But now you have this amazing new hockey team, right? And even though you can't play, you can be there in the thick of things, every single day."

"Speaking of which…I have a meeting I can't get out of. How would you feel about a quick forty-eight-hour trip to Florida?"

She sighed and looked down. "I can't."

"How come? Really, it would be quick and we could—"

"I don't have a passport."

"Oh." Damn, that sucked. I traveled back and forth between Canada and the US so much, it never occurred to me that some people didn't have passports. I knew it intellectually, but I'd never met anyone who didn't.

"I'm sorry."

"It's okay." I squeezed her hand, trying to think of something to say. "Maybe then I won't go…maybe I'll fly him out here."

"What?" She frowned in confusion.

"I want to sit down in person with the guy we want as head coach of the Knights, and we were going to do it in Fort Lauderdale. However, if you can't go, and we have so little time together as it is, maybe I'll just fly him to Vancouver."

"Oh, don't do that just because of me."

"I want to. I'm honestly dreading heading down to Florida. I'm excited about the team, but it's been nice being here in Garland Grove. Everything moves at a slower pace, like life is busy and the holidays are bustling, but things are relaxed. I don't know how to describe it. In my world, everything moves at breakneck speed, whether it's a business deal or a TV interview or back-to-back meetings about the new team. It never stops. And yet, here in Garland Grove, even though I'm still keeping up with everything online and via email, it's not like that."

"There's something to be said for small-town living," she said, nodding. "Most of the time, it's wonderful. People care about each other, traffic is nonexistent, there are a lot of old-fashioned values and very little crime. On the flip side of that, work is hard to find some-times. There's no major airport nearby so travel is a hassle. And everybody is in your business—like with our relationship and me having to consider what other people think. Mostly, I don't care, but you know what I mean."

I nodded. "I don't think I could live here full-time, but this would be the perfect place for a vacation home. And I'd love to spend holidays here."

"Best of both worlds," she said softly.

I wanted to tell her she could come with me, live with me, figure out where things were going, but it felt soon. It had been a little over a week. What the hell was wrong with me?

"I'm going to try to get Toli to fly to Vancouver instead of Fort Lauderdale," I said instead.

"Are you talking about Anatoli Petrov?" she asked, her eyes wide.

"Yeah. Are you a fan?"

"Hell yeah. I mean, he's legendary. I loved watching him play, especially after he was traded to Vegas. And then when he played his first pro game with his son...I don't think there was a dry eye at the bar that night. It was pretty epic seeing him and Anton on the ice together."

"You wanna meet him?"

She flashed me another huge grin. "Duh."

"I'm going to call him in the morning and see if I can set up an interview in person." I turned and started skating backwards, taking both her hands and pulling her closer to me. "In the meantime, is this the rink that's supposed to be magical?"

She laughed. "It is."

"What happens when you skate on it?"

"I'm not sure what's supposed to happen, because I've skated on this ice a million times and so far, nothing magical has happened."

"Until tonight."

She arched a brow. "What happened tonight?"

"This is the first time I've ever skated with a woman I'm involved with. Not counting random teenage stuff."

"Is that magical?"

"It is to me. To have a woman I really like, that also enjoys hockey and ice-skating, the two things I love most in the world, yeah, that's pretty magical."

She leaned forward, tilting up her face for a kiss, and I slowed down as I pressed my lips to hers. She was so damn sweet, it was kind of magical to kiss her right here on the ice, while skating, with Christmas music playing and white, red, and green lights flashing all around us.

"I'm a very lucky man," I whispered against her mouth as we glided to a stop.

"Tonight, I'm a very lucky woman," she whispered back.

"I'd like to take you to bed, sweetheart." I looked into her eyes, loving the way she gazed up at me.

She slowly pulled her lower lip through her teeth. "Me too. But I'd like to keep skating for a while, if that's okay? I love being here at the holidays."

"I'd love to keep skating for a while." I put some distance between us again and picked up speed, pulling her along with me. Despite not having been on skates in probably six months, I'd been skating for as long as I could remember and my body remembered what to do. I wasn't in hockey shape, but I was in excellent shape overall, and I wove in and out of slower skaters without slowing down.

With the wind blowing Noelle's hair out behind her, her cheeks flushed from both exertion and the cold, I would never forget the sheer joy emanating from her. And I never wanted it to end.

CHAPTER SIXTEEN

Noelle

I'd never had as much fun as I was having tonight with Remy. We skated for what felt like forever, going fast, slowing down, holding hands, talking and laughing like we'd known each other forever instead of a little over a week. I was falling hard and fast, which was one of the more ridiculous things I'd ever done, but the last couple of years hadn't been kind to me. My life could be summed up with the saying "if it wasn't for bad luck, I'd have no luck at all."

Remy breathed new life into me. I'd never been the type of woman who thought she needed a man to save her, but when I was with him, I didn't need saving. I'd never met anyone like him; gorgeous, famous, successful, hard-working, and more than anything else, kind. Thoughtful. Gentle. I'd even go so far as to describe him as loving. I'd had very little of any of that in my life and spent most of it kicking and clawing my way to survive. With Remy, I didn't have to do anything but live.

For the first time in my twenty-seven years on earth, I felt alive.

"When we're done here, you want to get a late dinner?" he asked me when we finally sat down to take a break.

I shook my head.

"No?" He seemed confused.

"Let's get takeout and go to bed."

"I like the way you think." He leaned over to kiss me and my mouth opened of its own volition. I couldn't help myself when we were together. No one had ever made me feel so beautiful. So desirable. So happy.

Happy wasn't a word I used often, but it had been a constant since Remy had arrived in Garland Grove.

I leaned against his side and he slid his arm around me, pulling me closer. He radiated heat and I soaked it in. I was so used to being cold, or at least chilly, that heat was a luxury. It was addictive and a little scary.

"You two are adorable," Tandy said, sinking down beside me. "But it's time to get everyone out of here, clean up, and go home."

"I think it was the busiest one yet," I said, looking around.

She nodded. "Over three hundred people showed up."

"Last year we topped out at one-ninety," I said. "So that's a good increase."

"But how much did we spend on hot chocolate and popcorn?" Remy asked.

"I know how many packages of cocoa I used," I said. "But I'll need to check inventory for the amount of popcorn. Then we'll get a number. But we absolutely broke even, and this isn't about making money; it's about the holidays and community fellowship and goodwill."

"That's all well and good," Remy said, "but this is a business. Sure, we can do something like this once or twice a year for all those reasons, but the rest of the year, it needs to be about profit."

"Is the rink profitable?" Tandy asked curiously.

"I've been looking at the numbers, and it is, but money seems to just disappear. There are expenses I don't understand, which makes me think my dad had money being taken out and put directly into one of his accounts. I still haven't sorted them all out, but my accountant is working on that now."

"Is that bad?" I asked carefully.

"It's not bad, but now that I own the place, I don't need the money and I'd rather it go back into the business or at the very least, to the employees."

"Does that mean you're not going to sell it?" Tandy asked, meeting his gaze without hesitation.

"I don't know." Remy's arm tightened around my shoulder. "I haven't been in town that long, but it feels so familiar here, like the rink and the town are one and the same."

"And it's hard to think about selling the soul of a town," Tandy said softly.

"Exactly."

We were all quiet for a few seconds as his words sunk in.

"Well, time to get everyone out of here." Tandy got up and started shooing skaters off the ice.

I lifted one of the urns of hot chocolate and Remy grabbed the other one. They were both almost empty and we brought them into the small kitchen behind the concession stand.

"If you'll go get the rest of the stuff," I told him, "I'll wash these."

"Okay."

He disappeared and I dumped out the urns, absently turning on the water and grabbing a sponge. I was lost in thought, wondering when Remy had begun to think of the rink as the soul of the town. I didn't even think of it that way, but now that Tandy had said it, it made sense. Somewhere along the way, I'd stopped seeing the magic of Garland Grove, the rink, and even the holidays. I didn't believe in magic, literally, figuratively or any other way. But when I was with Remy, there was always something magical brewing just beneath the surface. If I could bottle it, I'd probably be richer than he was. Since I couldn't, I had to settle for enjoying the magical time we were having together.

———

We went back to Vancouver the following Monday. We were spending the night again, and he'd invited Anatoli Petrov and his wife Tessa to town. The guys were meeting this afternoon while Tessa and I went shopping. I was completely out of my element, but Remy had asked me to hang out with her while they had their meeting, and I couldn't very well say no.

"What do I tell her about our relationship?" I asked Remy as we waited for them to arrive at our hotel suite.

"I don't know." He met my gaze. "The truth? That we've just met but can't seem to keep our eyes, hands, and mouths off each other?"

I snickered. "Yeah, okay, I'll lead with that."

"Just be honest. It's new. We don't know yet."

I nodded, nervously running my hands down my dark gray leggings. I hadn't worn anything but jeans or sweats in so long, I'd forgotten what it was like to get dressed up. Luckily, I'd been able to dig these ribbed leggings, a cute red sweater, and low-heeled boots out of one of my suitcases so I looked presentable.

I was nervous but super excited about meeting one of my all-time favorite hockey players. Remy said Toli was incredibly down-to-earth and not to worry. I still did, of course, until the knock came on the door and the tall Russian and his wife came in. Toli was about six-two, and lean and fit, with cropped blond hair and a twinkle in his blue eyes that instantly put me at ease. Tessa was shorter, about my height, with curly blond hair and a friendly smile.

"I have a car waiting to take you and Noelle shopping and wherever else you want to go today," Remy told Tessa once we'd all been introduced. "And then we'll meet at a restaurant downtown at seven. Does that sound okay?"

"Anything that involves shopping and food is good with me," Tessa said, smiling up at her husband.

He leaned down and lightly kissed her. "See you later."

"See you later."

Tessa and I headed down to the car. He was pulling out all the stops because he really wanted Toli to be his new head coach, but they had four young children at home, and they weren't sure that moving away from everyone and everything they knew was the best choice for their family. Remy was going to use today to change his mind, and had asked me to be as positive as possible. Since I'd never been to Fort Lauderdale and didn't know much about the new team, I couldn't offer any personal experience, but I could talk about what a good guy Remy was. And that, at least, was a hundred percent the truth.

"Can we start at the Coach store?" Tessa asked me. "I need a new bag and haven't had time to shop lately."

"Sure. We can go wherever you want. I'm not a big shopper."

She glanced at me. "No?"

"I've been broke since graduating college, and before you ask, Remy and I are really new together, so I'm not down with letting him buy me things."

"I see. How new is new?"

I grimaced. "Two weeks."

"And he's already bringing you along to big meetings like this? It must be pretty intense."

"Yeah, it really is. It's a little scary *how* intense it is."

"Toli and I fell hard and fast too," she mused. "And look at us now. Five kids and—"

"You have *five* kids?" I wrinkled my nose. "That sounds exhausting."

"Well, that includes Toli's son from another relationship, Anton, who's an adult, so he doesn't live with us. And it also includes my daughter, Raina, from my first marriage. She'll be nine next month. Then we have the babies, the three boys Toli and I had together. Alex, Andy, and AJ."

"Raina must be the princess as the only girl," I said, grinning.

Tessa laughed. "She rules the roost, no doubt about it. Has Toli wrapped around her little finger."

"That sounds nice."

"He's a great dad. He loves all our kids fiercely. I got so lucky when I met him at that bar seven years ago."

"Only seven years?" I asked. "Seems like you've been together much longer."

"Well, second marriage for me, and he was almost thirty-five when we met, so we felt like we needed to play catch-up with babies and marriage and all that."

"I'm only twenty-seven, so I'm in no rush, but honestly, I don't think Remy's in a rush for something serious either. And he's thirty-five."

"You never know," she said. "Toli was ready to settle down, but he said he waited to meet the right woman. It could very well be the same for Remy."

"I don't know. He's leaving for Florida right after Christmas and I'm staying here, so I don't think we have much potential for a future together and after dating for two whole weeks, I'm not comfortable bringing it up."

"That makes sense."

"He's brought up doing a long-distance thing for a while, and that's good for me." I paused. "What about you? Do you want to move to Fort Lauderdale?"

She sighed. "It's so hard. Toli's only been retired a little over a year but he's antsy, restless, and working part-time as a scout for the Sidewinders isn't cutting it for him. I know he wants this job, but it means a lot of extra work for me. In Vegas, I have a huge support system. In Florida, I'll have no one. And it's different when you're the coach's wife. As a player's wife, it was easy. The WAGs all stick together."

"WAGs?"

"Wives and girlfriends."

"Oh."

"As the coach's wife, I have to be a little more aloof, a little distant, because it could get complicated for him. He's also fairly young to be a head coach. So the assistant coaches' wives are much older than me, and none of them have young kids. I mean, AJ is only two."

"I understand. So are you going to decline the offer?"

She met my gaze. "You're saying Remy is going to offer him the job today?"

I nodded since it wasn't a secret. "Yes."

"He says he won't take it if I don't want him to, but I know how badly he wants this, so it boils down to compromise and sacrifice. Raina isn't happy about the prospect, but the littles won't know any better. The hardest part for Toli, I think, is being away from Anton."

"Anton plays for the Sidewinders, right?"

Tessa nodded. "Yes, but I think if Remy offers Toli the job, we're going to take it because even though it'll be harder for me, I love him enough to want him to be happy."

"I hope he appreciates you," I said softly.

"Oh, he does. He's..." Her voice trailed off and she smiled. "Honestly, he's the absolute love of my life, the greatest man I know. He'll do anything for me. Including give up this job. But I don't want that for him."

"I hope someone loves me like that someday," I said after a moment.

"You may have already found him."

I didn't dare say that I hoped so out loud because I didn't want to jinx anything.

Was Remy love-of-my-life-soulmate material?

CHAPTER SEVENTEEN

Remy

"Tell me all the negatives," I told Toli after we'd talked. "Give me a chance to change your mind."

"It's not my mind that needs changing," he said quietly. "My wife has been through a lot and by moving, I go back to not being home much and ultimately taking away her support system. I don't know if I can do that to her after what happened with our youngest son's birth."

I cocked my head. "Dare I ask?"

"I was on a road trip when she went into labor. She'd been having some weird complications and asked me not to go, but her OB said everything was okay, so I went. She collapsed, started to hemorrhage, and had to have an emergency hysterectomy. Meanwhile, I'm stuck in Chicago in a blizzard, and didn't get home until the following day. My buddy from the team, Zakk Cloutier, was home with an injury, and he's the one who found her and got her to the hospital. So even though we're done having kids, I don't know how I feel about putting her in the position where something might happen and she'll be alone."

"She'll never be alone," I said firmly. "I'm not going on the road with you guys, so I'll be around. All she has to do is call. And I mean that."

"I appreciate that." Toli leaned back in his chair. "What it boils down to is, the one thing I've learned about marriage is that it has to be a two-way street, and so far, it's been her making all the big sacrifices for me. Unless she's on board, I can't give you an answer. Believe me, I want this so bad I can taste it, but at some point, I have to do what's right for my family. I missed most of Anton's childhood because of hockey, and this time around, I want to be a hands-on dad. But the pull to be in the hockey world is strong as fuck."

I chuckled. "Believe me, I've been retired five years and I still miss it. Every fucking day."

"Well, if you have any ideas on how to convince Tessa this is a good thing for our family, I'm all ears."

"The hockey lifestyle isn't easy," I said. "That's partly why I stayed single while I was playing. But if you want the job, I'll bend over backwards to make the deal attractive to Tessa. Just tell me what will motivate her."

"I don't know." Toli's eyes were shrouded as he looked down. "She's not motivated by money, and you can't sign all of her friends' husbands."

"Maybe not all of them, but if you give me some names, I can make at least one of them happen."

"You drive a hell of a bargain, Mr. Knight."

"I go after the things I want, and right now, what I want is you as the head coach of my hockey team."

"Then you'll need to pick up either Zakk Cloutier or Karl Martensson."

I grimaced. "Jesus. Martensson's one of the best goalies in the world —you think the Sidewinders will let him go?"

Toli shrugged. "That, my friend, is not my job."

"Let's see what I can do."

We met up with the ladies about an hour later and it looked like they'd become fast friends. They were chatting about something Tessa had bought and only stopped long enough to say hello.

"I'm starving," Tessa announced. "All that shopping made me hungry."

"I'm hungry too," Noelle agreed, opening the menu.

I'd chosen a high-end steakhouse, both because it was expected in a meeting like this and also because I wanted to spoil Noelle. She normally resisted going to the nicer restaurants, and I suspected it had to do with her not having the right clothes to wear, but regardless, we were here tonight. It wasn't an overly fancy place, but the steaks were some of the best on the west coast and it was one of my favorite restaurants in Vancouver.

"Remington Knight, you are in *so* much trouble."

I spun around at the sound of my name and all but gaped at my mother.

"Mom." I quickly got to my feet, hugging her. "Hi."

"You didn't tell me you were in Vancouver. *Again.*" She gave me a pointed glare.

"This is business, Mom." I turned to the table. "Mom, please meet the man I hope will be the new head coach of the Lauderdale Knights, Anatoli Petrov, and his wife Tessa."

"Hello, so nice to meet you." My mother was the ultimate lady, especially once I mentioned business. She might rag on me in private, but her public face would be nothing but polite sophistication. They all shook hands and then I held out a hand to Noelle, who got to her feet as she took it.

"This is Noelle Burrier," I told my mother. "Noelle, my mother, Aletha Knight."

"It's very nice to meet you." I saw the nervousness in Noelle's eyes, but she smiled and shook my mother's hand.

"Would you like to join us?" I asked politely, even though I prayed she would say no.

"Of course not. You're with friends." She smiled. "Anyway, I have a date."

"A date." I stared at her as if I hadn't heard her right.

"A date. You know, like the thing you're on…" She motioned to Noelle. "Anyway, I hope you'll come home with Remy for Christmas, Noelle. I'd love to get to know you better."

"I'm not sure what our plans are yet but thank you so much for the invitation." Noelle nodded.

"I'll call you tomorrow." My mother lifted her cheek for a kiss, which I gave her, and then she sauntered across the restaurant, where a handsome man of about sixty got up and kissed her hello.

"I had no idea my mother was dating," I murmured, sinking back in my chair.

Toli chuckled. "I can't imagine my mother dating. My father is still alive, but I mean in general. I think I'd be so overprotective she'd kill me."

"Good thing she's in Russia then." Tessa gave him a teasing smile.

"So, shall we order wine?"

———

"Do you think he's going to take the job?" Noelle asked me late that night after we'd made love and were just about to drop off to sleep.

"I don't know," I admitted, wrapping my arms around her. "He wants it, but he's worried about Tessa."

"She's going to say yes," I said softly. "She already told me that his happiness is more important than hers. So to speak."

"Really?"

She nodded in the darkness. "Yeah. I think they're the sweetest couple. She loves him so much you can hear it in her voice when she talks about him."

"I think he's deeply in love with her too," I said. "Though I'm probably not as in tune to that kind of thing as you ladies are."

"Trust me—he's going to say yes."

"Well, that's makes me pretty damn happy." I paused. "But did you get the vibe that she's going to be miserable?"

"No. I got the vibe that she'll do whatever she has to do to make her husband happy, within reason."

"I got the same vibe. He told me there are two players whose wives she's extremely close to, so I'm going after at least one of them either in the expansion draft or as a trade afterwards."

"You could also try to get his son," she said thoughtfully.

"Anton's young and the Sidewinders drafted him. There are a lot of rules about younger players. I'd have to see what I could possibly offer them that would make them give up a young star like Anton."

"There are rules, but there are always ways around the rules," she replied. "And if you want Toli as your head coach, I think you might want to do whatever you can to get him."

"He and I would have to talk about that because I don't know how a father-son relationship would work with him as head coach."

"Something to think about, though."

"You have quite the head for hockey," I said. "You want to work in the back office with me?"

"I'd like to be Director of Hockey Operations," she said without missing a beat. "If you can make that happen, sure."

"Damn, woman, you drive a hard bargain."

"Damn straight."

I leaned over to kiss her bare shoulder. "I like that about you."

"So was your mom really annoyed you didn't tell her you were in Vancouver?"

"Probably a little, but not actually mad about it. She knows I'm busy and when she met Toli, she instantly understood that this was an important meeting. She knows I want him as my head coach."

"Don't you have to clear it with other people in the organization?" she asked.

"Yes and no. The others—my current Director of Hockey Operations—and the General Manager, already went through two rounds of interviews with him. My two investors aren't interested in the day-to-day details, so that's all me. Plus I own fifty-two percent of the team, and they each only own twenty-four. That was done by design so I always have the final say."

"Do you think bringing one of Tessa's friends along will sweeten the deal for them?"

"It definitely will, but both of the players Toli mentioned will be tough to get. Probably even harder than picking up Anton. I mean, Zakk Cloutier is at the height of his career. He's thirty-one now, thirty-two next season, so I'd say he has three or four good years left. And Karl Martensson is the starting goalie for the Sidewinders. He's thirty-four, so thirty-five next season, which puts him closer to the end of his career. They'd want a fortune for either of those guys, and while Zakk would probably be a great addition no matter how much money we spend, I don't know that a thirty-five-year-old goalie with only a few years left is the direction we want to go."

"You bring on someone huge to start, though," she said. "Name recognition, a strong leader in the locker room, and then have an up-and-coming young backup who'll hopefully be ready to take over once Karl retires."

I leaned over and rested my chin on her shoulder. "Miles Hammond, my Director of Hockey Operations, is going to hate you."

"Why?" she asked, chuckling.

"Because I'm thinking of actually firing him and hiring you in his place."

"I'm not ready for anything like that." She turned over so we were facing each other. "But I love hockey and I'll talk about it all day long, anytime you want."

"I always want." I kissed her, my lips touching hers gently. "Except when I want to do this." I slid my hand along the curve of her hip. "And this." I nibbled the soft spot behind her ear. "And maybe this." My hand moved to the apex between her thighs.

"I like those things too." She sighed against my mouth.

"You wanna go again?"

"You don't even have to ask."

"I'll always ask, but I love knowing the answer will be yes."

CHAPTER EIGHTEEN

Noelle

Toli and Tessa stayed an extra day and the four of us did some touristy things the following day, walking around the city, taking a ferry ride, and having dinner at another high-end restaurant. Tessa and I had exchanged numbers, and though it felt a little surreal to me, it was nice to have a new friend. Though I didn't show it on the outside, I was also completely flabbergasted that I was now friends with one of my hockey heroes.

Toli was as laid-back as Remy said he was, but he was way funnier than I'd anticipated, and he had us all in stitches as he told stories about the kids, his hockey career, and life on the road. Remy had fun stories too and we sat at the restaurant for hours, long after we'd finished dinner, dessert, after-dinner cocktails and several bottles of wine.

"We have an early flight," Toli said as things started to wrap up. "But we wanted to tell you before we left that we've decided to make the move to Fort Lauderdale."

"I'm really happy to hear that." Remy held out his hand and Toli shook it. Remy turned to Tessa and hugged her. "I'm going to make sure it's worth your while."

"Oh, you definitely will." She smiled playfully. "When one of the kids is sick and I haven't slept in three days and Toli's on the road, guess who I'm calling?"

Remy looked around, as if confused. "Uh, I don't know. Noelle?"

"Oh, I see how you are." I nudged him. "You talk the talk but then don't walk the walk."

"Fine." He blew out a breath as if annoyed, though there was no doubt he was joking because of the twinkle in his eyes. "I'll come babysit."

"Excellent." Tessa winked at me and after quick hugs from both her and Toli, they were gone.

"I really liked them," I told him as we got ready for bed.

"He's good people," Remy agreed. "And Tessa seems great as well. He's going to be an amazing addition to the organization, and I think having Tessa as the team matriarch, so to speak, will also be incredible. Someone like her, who's been a hockey wife for a long time, can help the younger WAGs get their feet under them. The nice thing about an expansion team is that even the veteran players will be new to the team, the arena, and the city, which makes for a much more level playing field for everyone."

"Sounds like it's going to be a really exciting time," I said softly, unable to keep the envy out of my voice.

But Remy heard it. "You'll come visit," he whispered, pulling me close. "As often as you can get away."

"I know."

"Let's get your passport taken care of before I leave, okay? I know you don't have a lot of extra money, so let me pay for it, please? You're only getting it so we can see each other as often as possible, so let me pay the fee."

"All right."

"I've been thinking about what my mom said, though. Why don't you come to Vancouver with me for Christmas?"

My eyes snapped up to his in surprise. I'd heard his mother suggest it, but hadn't thought he'd actually offer. Now he'd caught me off guard and I wasn't sure how to answer.

"You don't think it would be...awkward?" I asked at last.

He frowned. "Why? We're seeing each other and it's the holidays."

"We've been dating, like, ten minutes. If you bring me home for the holidays, your family will wonder how serious it is, and we don't know the answer to that."

"So? Do we need to know our five-year plan to enjoy Christmas together?"

"I don't have the money to buy gifts for anyone and before you say I don't have to, it's polite. I can't show up at your mother's for Christmas without at least a bottle of wine or flowers or something."

"Must you overthink everything?" he asked, lifting my chin so I was looking right up into his face. "I want you to be with me, to spend time with my mother and brothers, and for us to be together as much as possible until I have to go."

"I know, but I have to talk to Connie because we always spend Christmas together, you know? And Alex looks forward to me coming."

He sighed. "Connie has a fiancé and two kids and her own family. While I appreciate your loyalty to her, you have your own life. And frankly, why would you want to spend Christmas with Craig?" He wrinkled his nose distastefully at the mention of his name.

We chuckled together.

"Let me talk to Connie, okay?"

"Okay." He kissed the tip of my nose. "So, is this where I ask if you want to get naked?"

"If it is, this is where I tell you that you don't have to ask."

"And where I respond that I'll always ask because it's the gentlemanly thing to do."

"I love it when you talk gentleman to me."

The trip was great, and the only bummer was the whole Christmas situation. Connie would probably be hurt if I didn't spend the holidays with her, mostly because I was buffer for her and Craig, who tended to drink too much. And this year, none of us had any money. Part of me felt guilty, because I had the opportunity to be with the greatest guy I'd ever known, much less dated, and spend the holidays eating, drinking, and being merry while Connie would probably spend most of it tending to the kids and trying to put together a meal on almost no budget.

We hadn't talked in a couple of days, so I was surprised when Connie showed up at the arena with the kids on Friday afternoon while I was getting the concession stand stocked and ready for the Friday night high school game. Based on how red and puffy her eyes were, Connie had been crying, which meant she and Craig been fighting, and I just wanted to throat-punch him. He wasn't a bad guy, but he was lazy, uninspired, and simply not the right guy for Connie. She deserved someone who'd truly love and respect her, and now she had two kids with two different guys, neither of which did much to take care of her.

"What are you doing here?" I asked her as I handed Alexander a bag of cookies.

"Craig has a job interview at the garland factory," she said. "So we all came. I figured I could see you and maybe do a little bit of shopping.

Mr. Allston usually has a good clearance rack at his shop and there might be something for the kids."

"You think you guys will move back to Garland Grove?"

"If he gets the job, yes, because commuting forty minutes each way in winter sucks, and his truck is on its last leg."

"I hope he gets it."

"He's been really stressed about it. He didn't get it the last time he applied, but we heard through the grapevine there was an opening so he just showed up, hoping to get an interview on the spot. It's been kind of stressful."

"The holidays are stressful," I murmured, trying not to say anything negative about Craig. "But is everything okay?"

"Not really. It's always the same, you know? No money, no job, no nothing. Christmas is going to suck, we had to turn off the cable, and if things don't pick up, Internet will be next."

I sighed. "I can give you—"

"You've given me enough." She looked away. "I fucked up again, didn't I?"

I didn't want to kick someone who was already down, so I just shrugged. "We can't help who we love."

"But I *don't* love him," she muttered. "He was so good with Alex, he had a decent job when we met, and I thought I'd learn to love him. Then everything went to shit. God, I'm a mess." She swiped at her eyes.

"If you want to leave him, we can make it work," I whispered. "I should be set to get an apartment by June. We have six months to figure it out."

"I have two kids. What will I do with them while I work so I can pay my share of the rent?" she asked sadly.

"Alex will be in school all day next year, and if Remy gets me the raise he's promised, I can keep Daphne with me during the day. You could do something part-time maybe, just enough to buy groceries and pay utilities. I'll handle the rent and stuff. And Craig will have to pay child support, whether he wants to or not."

"With what? His good looks?" She scowled. "Damn, girlfriend, how did we wind up like this?"

"We're going to be fine," I told her firmly. "Whatever it takes, we're going to be okay."

"Two weeks ago I was lecturing you about not trying to make a better life for yourself, and look at me now, the pot calling the kettle black."

"Nothing is that black and white," I said gently. "You have kids to think about."

"Con!" Craig came stalking down the concourse, his face a mask of fury.

"How'd it go?" she asked, turning to him.

"Fuckers didn't want me," he grunted. "Fucking prejudiced assholes. They said I didn't have enough experience."

"Well, you don't," I pointed out.

He gave me a dirty look. "Oh, shut up, will you, Noelle? At least I'm not homeless."

"At least I have a job and a college degree," I shot back.

"Stop it." Connie had tears in her eyes. "Both of you. This isn't helping."

"Hey, guys." Remy came walking down the hall and Connie quickly turned away, swiping at her eyes.

Remy and I exchanged glances as he took in the tense situation, but I gave a slight shake of my head, hoping he hadn't heard Craig's comment about me being homeless and indicating he shouldn't comment.

"We probably need to get going," Craig muttered, not even acknowledging Remy.

Remy didn't seem to notice, or at least was pretending like he didn't, and turned to all of us. "What do you say we go out for a late dinner? My treat."

"It's getting late," Connie murmured. "The kids have to go to bed."

"Why?" I asked her. "It's not like they have to be at work in the morning. Come on, let's go get some food."

"I could eat," Craig said, perking up a little at the offer, which just made me hate him more.

"Have you figured out if you're going to hire anyone else?" I asked Remy as we headed out to the parking lot. Craig and Connie were going to meet us at a diner not too far from here.

"Not yet. Why?"

"Connie really needs a job, and a place where she can bring the kids if she has to."

"I haven't figured out the details yet," he said, "but let me think about it. I'm going to talk to my accountant tomorrow to go over the numbers and then I'll know more. Okay?"

"Thank you. I appreciate how kind you are to her, especially when Craig is such a dick."

"Guys like him..." he shook his head. "Well, she definitely deserves better."

"She knows it too. If she can find a job here in Garland Grove, she might move back and we can get a place together, without Craig."

He opened his mouth but then closed it again. I wanted to ask what he'd been about to say but figured it would bring up topics I wasn't comfortable with. Like my living situation, which was strictly off-limits conversation-wise.

"I get the feeling he's not going to give her up that easily," he said after a moment.

"You think?" I glanced over at him.

"He just strikes me as the kind of guy who won't respond well to her leaving."

"That's what I'm afraid of," I admitted.

CHAPTER NINETEEN

Remy

Dinner was mostly a stilted affair, with Craig bitching nonstop about the garland factory's refusal to hire him and Connie dealing with both kids. Craig was one of those guys who gave the rest of us a bad reputation. He had no interest in either of the kids, not even his own, and ordered three beers before our food even arrived. I couldn't think of anyone who'd annoyed me more than Craig in years, and it took a lot of self-control not to tell him exactly what I thought of him.

Noelle did her best to engage with Alexander and talk about random things, just to keep things light, but Craig was nothing if not tenacious, consistently bad-mouthing the garland factory.

"What was your last job?" I asked him.

"Another factory, but I hurt my back so I can't really go back there."

"Well, if you told them about your back, the factory probably thought you weren't a good risk."

"I had to tell them why I haven't worked in so long," Craig protested. "I couldn't just say there's no reason I've been mostly out of work for a year."

"Right, but did you tell them it's all better now?"

Craig swallowed and then took a swig of beer. "Nah. I figured I'd be honest, so maybe they'd put me in an office instead of in the back. I can't lift boxes and shit, you know?"

"But isn't that the position your interview was for?" I countered.

He gave me a dirty look. "Yeah, but how else am I supposed to get a job? If I lie, and then can't do the job, they're going to fire me anyway."

"Well, if you can't do the job, why would you apply?"

"Oh, fuck off, man." Craig rolled his eyes. "I need a fucking job. Not everyone is a goddamn billionaire."

I sighed. Why did everyone think I was a billionaire? I mean, I did well, but not that well.

"I worked harder than most people ever work in their entire lives," I said simply. "But when that heart attack took me out of hockey, I busted my ass all over again to get my sporting goods business off the ground. Don't mistake my wealth for luck because I've worked my fucking ass off to be where I am."

Craig rolled his eyes. "Yeah, whatever. All you pro athletes have it easy. I'd kill to do what you do."

"Well, you needed to start at around six years old and give up most of your teenage years. And even then, only about one percent of us make it to the NHL."

Craig downed the rest of his beer and motioned to the waitress to bring another.

"So, are you coming on the twenty-fourth and sleeping over?" Connie asked Noelle.

"Oh, um, I hadn't gotten that far yet," Noelle murmured, not looking at me.

"That's usually our plan, but I wasn't sure if Remy would still be here?" Connie looked over at me, a question in her eyes.

"I'm going to be in Vancouver with my mom and brothers," I said quietly, though I was a little annoyed that Noelle had apparently made her decision about Christmas without even talking to me.

"Noelle makes the absolute best prime rib," Connie said. "It's the most amazing meal we eat all year."

"We don't have money for prime rib," Craig muttered, picking up the burger that had just been put in front of him. "We don't even have money for hotdogs. We should go to my stepdad's for Christmas. At least they'll feed us."

"Your stepdad smokes pot in the house," Connie said. "I'm not bringing the kids over there."

Craig rolled his eyes. "Yeah, okay, Ms. Goody Two-shoes. I don't know how I got stuck with a prude like you."

Connie's mouth dropped open and then she snapped it shut.

"What's a prune, Mommy?" Alexander asked.

"It's a fruit," she said tightly. "But Daddy's just joking. Anyway, what do you want Santa to bring you this year?"

The conversation switched to everything Alexander had on his holiday list, and I ate my dinner in relative silence. Noelle hadn't looked at me since the comment about Christmas and I figured she could sense my annoyance. I was trying to be patient, but we had so little time left together and without a passport, who knew how long it would be until she could come visit me in Florida.

Unless she didn't want to.

It occurred to me that maybe I was far more into her than she was into me. Maybe that's why she was so reluctant to let me buy her things and do nice things for her. She liked me, but didn't see a future for us, and was just enjoying the fun and sex we were having until I left.

I'd never been in a position like this before, where I was falling head over heels for a woman who was determined to keep me at arm's length. Yes, we spent time together and couldn't keep our hands off each other, but whenever we talked about the future, families, when we'd see each other again, she tended to get quiet. I'd thought by inviting her to Christmas she'd see my feelings for her, but maybe not. Maybe her goals in life didn't include being with a washed-up, albeit rich, retired hockey player, moving to an intracoastal town, and living and breathing hockey for the foreseeable future.

Maybe she wanted a simpler guy. Someone who'd pay more attention to her than I would once hockey season got underway. Someone who'd put her first. And that probably wasn't me.

Was it?

I was in a pretty bad mood by the time Connie, Craig, and the kids took off, and Noelle and I headed out.

"Are you mad at me?" she asked once we were in the SUV. "You haven't said five words in the last hour."

I shrugged. "Not mad. Maybe a little disappointed."

"Disappointed?" She cocked her head.

"Christmas, Noelle. You made the decision not to spend it with me without even another discussion, and frankly, that kind of tells me I'm not a priority in your life."

"First of all, Connie caught me by surprise—I haven't had a chance to talk to her about it yet—and I didn't want to have any kind of conversation in front of Craig. I haven't decided anything, but if we're being honest, how can I make you a priority? You're leaving tomorrow and it's probably going to be months before we see each other again, if at all."

"If at all?" I turned toward her. "What does that mean?"

"It just means I'm realistic."

"About what? Us seeing each other again? You think that little of me, that I'd offer to pay your passport fees specifically so you can come visit me, and then just disappear?"

"You wouldn't be the first guy who did something like that, and that's one of the reasons I'm reluctant about spending Christmas with you and your family. We don't know if we're going to see each other again, and getting to know your family will just make it that much harder when we say goodbye."

"Wow." That hurt. I figured she must have a history with men who had treated her badly, but I deserved better because I'd bent over backwards to show her I wasn't like that. I wanted to see where this thing with us was going, but now it felt strikingly apparent that it wasn't going anywhere.

"I'm sorry," she said after a moment. "I feel like we've gotten our wires crossed."

"I feel like you've written us off without even giving us a chance," I said. "But that's okay. I'm leaving for Vancouver tomorrow and I guess I'll head straight to Florida after Christmas."

"You're not coming back?" she asked after a slight hesitation.

I pulled into the arena parking lot, since that's where she'd left her car. "I was going to, but I think maybe you're right, that it's better not to get too involved."

"What about the arena?" she asked.

"I don't know. I'm going to make some decisions once I get to my mom's and I'll let you know."

A strange, awkward silence filled the air and neither of us moved or said anything for at least a couple of minutes.

"So is this...goodbye?" she asked, her voice a whisper.

"That's up to you."

"Can you...I mean, can we, um, take a couple of days to think? I don't want it to end this way."

I didn't want it to end at all, but I was tired of chasing her. At some point, she needed to let me catch her because this game was getting old. It had only been about twenty days, so not even three full weeks, but I'd thought we had something special. Either she didn't agree or there was something in her life keeping her from letting herself be with me.

I reached out and took her hand. "I don't know what your secrets are, or why you've refused to truly open up to me, but I think at this point you have a decision to make."

"What decision?" She was staring down at our linked hands.

"Do you want to try or not." I held up a finger when she started to respond. "Just think about it. I'll call you in a couple of days and we can talk if you want to. But if you decide you do want to talk things out, you have to tell me everything. All the things you've kept bottled up, all the secrets you're too stubborn to share. Either we're in it or we're not; there's no in-between."

She looked up and her big green eyes were filled with tears. "I'm sorry," she whispered.

"Me too." I brushed the tears away with my knuckles. "Don't cry, okay? It's not a bad thing to do a little soul-searching."

"Okay."

I leaned over and brushed my lips across her forehead. "I'll wait until you're in your car."

"I left my bag inside, so I've got to go get it," she said. "You don't have to wait."

"Okay." I watched her get out of the SUV and walk into one of the back doors of the arena.

I started to pull away but instead of turning onto the street, I pulled off and parked in a lot across the street where I could see her car. I was annoyed and disappointed, but still curious as fuck. What could be so bad that she would push me away like this? I'd had a few minutes of self-doubt earlier, but we were too good together for her to walk away like she had, without a backward glance.

Was she married? Living with someone?

It didn't seem likely since the whole town knew we'd been together, but maybe if I followed her home, I'd get a feel for what was going on. I couldn't understand why she was so reluctant to give me—*us*—a chance. She'd been okay until the Christmas thing came up and then she'd absolutely panicked. If there was a correlation between her secrets and the holidays, I couldn't put it together without more information, hence my sitting here like a freakin' stalker. I just wanted to help, to do whatever it took for us to maybe have a future. Because I cared about her more than I wanted to admit.

But she didn't come back out and after two hours had passed, I decided to text her.

REMY: Hey. Just wanted to check in, make sure you were okay.

NOELLE: I just got into bed. We'll talk in a day or two.

Why the fuck would she lie to me about being in bed when she was still at the arena? There was no one else there, and when we'd left earlier, she'd cleaned everything up so she couldn't be working.

I sat there until three in the morning, and Noelle never left.

It was the oddest feeling, sitting there watching for her, knowing she was there when she'd told me she was at home. I couldn't figure out why she would lie. I refused to believe she was married, so something else was going on.

And then it hit me like a ton of bricks.

Sonofabitch.

CHAPTER TWENTY

Noelle

I took a lukewarm shower, bundled myself in three layers of clothes, and curled up in my old sleeping bag. It was weatherproof, so it kept me pretty warm, but it had gotten so cold the last few days. And I'd gotten used to sleeping with Remy, who was like my own personal heater. I'd forgotten how much I disliked being cold until I'd spent most of the last three weeks sleeping in warm beds. With a warm, sexy man I was already half in love with.

I tossed and turned all night, partly because I was cold and partly because I felt like hell after saying goodbye to Remy. He was such a good guy and I was being an insecure twit. In my heart of hearts, this was all my fault. I should have called Remy and apologized, should have told him that I didn't want anything more than to spend Christmas with him, to spend my life with him. But past hurts, pride, and insecurity were strong emotions to fight individually, much less all three at once.

My financial and living situations shouldn't have been such a big deal, but they were. No matter how many times I reminded myself I was almost at my goal, that I wouldn't be homeless much longer, reality somehow managed to rear up and smack me in the face. Remy was so hardworking, focused, and successful, I couldn't let him see how low I'd let myself fall.

Six months, I reminded myself when I finally got up and changed into the warmest clothes I owned.

The plan was to be in some kind of apartment, even a small room somewhere by June first. Maybe sooner if I got the raise Remy promised me.

I groaned as I thought about that.

There was no way I'd ask him about it now that we were on the outs, but if he sold the arena out from under me, I'd need some kind of warning. Which meant we had to talk at least once more.

I brushed my teeth, put my hair in a ponytail and slid my feet into my boots. The arena had been colder than usual last night, so I needed to check the thermostat. Then I might go sit at the library for a while because everything about the arena reminded me of Remy.

My phone rang and I sighed when I saw Connie's name on the screen.

"Hey."

"Hey." She sounded subdued.

"What's going on?"

"Craig and I had another fight and he left around three in the morning. He hasn't come back."

"That sounds like a good thing to me." I was usually more tactful with Connie, but I was done with pussyfooting around the issues with Craig.

"Yeah, I know."

"What are you going to do?"

"I don't know. Nothing until after the holidays."

"Well, Remy and I had a fight last night too."

"Oh, no. Why?"

I told her what happened.

"It's my fault," she groaned. "I never should have brought up Christmas until we were alone."

"It's all right. It was inevitable, you know? He's leaving soon and chances are, he's going to forget all about me."

"Maybe. But maybe not. You should have more faith in yourself. Remy seems like a good guy. If he was interested in me? I'd be all over it. Even if I wound up with a broken heart, he's the kind of guy most of us only dream of. You've met an actual knight in shining armor and you keep pretending he's the enemy."

"It's not that he's the enemy," I said gently. "He's just a fantasy. A one-night stand that turned into a few weeks, but we both know it's not going anywhere."

"He invited you to spend the holidays with his *family*. Are you kidding right now? You think he would do that if he didn't plan to keep seeing you?"

"How can I do that?" I cried in frustration. "Oh, hey, let me hop on a plane to Florida where I can visit my millionaire boyfriend. Then I'll come back to Garland Grove so I can continue sleeping in a sleeping bag on the floor of the women's locker room! He would probably die of embarrassment if he found out."

Connie was quiet for a few seconds. "He still doesn't know you're basically living at the arena?"

"No and he better not find out either. There's only so many hits my pride can take. It's exhausting trying to be strong all the time and letting him see how badly life has beaten me down isn't an option."

"Noelle, are you listening to yourself? He's the perfect person to help you get back on your feet."

"I'm not a freakin' prostitute!" I snapped.

"Oh my god. Stop it, okay? There's nothing about dating a great guy who happens to have money that makes you a *whore*. You're smart and educated and hardworking. You ran into a serious string of bad luck but you've almost pulled yourself out of it. No one who cares about you would ever look down on you."

"What makes you think he cares about me? He could have anyone!"

"That's right. He can have absolutely anyone. So why do you think he invited you to Christmas with his mother? To dump you the next day? That's ludicrous, even for you."

I sighed.

A lot of what she was saying rang true.

All of this was on me. My demons, my pride, my inability to trust.

"I guess it's moot now, though," I said after a minute. "He said he's leaving from Vancouver so I'm probably not going to see him again."

"Unless you call him and come clean."

"Not happening."

"Why? This is your chance to find something real. A man who loves you, maybe a family, someone who—"

"Stop!" I said, interrupting her. "Jesus. Would you listen to yourself? We've known each other three weeks. Twenty days to be exact. People don't fall in love that fast. Especially not guys like him."

"Says who?" she demanded. "You're falling for him, aren't you? Why can't he feel the same?"

"I don't know."

"Exactly. You don't know, but you're walking away before you can find out. That's your MO, how you try to protect yourself, but at the end of the day, can a broken heart be worse than what you're dealing with now?"

"And what happens to you if I run off with him?" I asked her.

"I'll figure it out. Just like you're figuring out your shit, I'm working on mine. I'm going to look for subsidized housing in Vancouver and in Garland Grove. Whichever comes up first, I'm leaving Craig and moving there. Then I'll get a job."

"I thought we were going to live together?" I asked in confusion.

"Maybe. But you have to make your plans without me. Just like you don't want anyone saving you, maybe I don't want anyone saving me."

"I thought it was different with us, you and me?"

"It is but it isn't. I have two kids now, and I have to get my shit together for them. Not for myself, not for you, but for *them*. And the first thing I have to do is leave Craig. Then find an affordable place to live and a decent job."

"I was trying to see if Remy would hire you at the arena but now I don't know if he's selling it or not."

"It's all right. Unlike Craig, I might be able to do that job at the garland factory. I just need someone to watch Daphne if I do because I don't think I can afford day care."

"I can help."

"I know, but you have your own stuff going on."

"I feel like you're purposely pushing me away so I'll run off with Remy," I said suspiciously.

"Maybe. One of us has to grow a pair, you know?"

I chuckled. "Look, let's just hang in there until the holidays are over. We'll reassess after the first of the year."

"Under one condition."

"What?" I asked warily.

"You call Remy."

"And say what?"

"Tell him the truth."

"No."

"Then I'm doing my thing without you."

"You're so full of shit," I muttered.

"No, I'm serious. Someone has to save you from yourself."

I rolled my eyes even though she couldn't see it.

"By the way, you might want to drive up here tonight."

"How come?"

"There's a blizzard coming. The news says it's going to be brutal."

"What?"

"Yeah, go online or turn on a weather channel. Supposed to hit tomorrow sometime. Looking at six feet of snow."

"What?! We don't get that much snow, especially not in December."

"I'm telling you—go look it up."

"Great. Like this day hasn't sucked enough. All right, I'm going to see what's what. I'll call you later if I'm going to drive up there."

"Okay. And call Remy."

"Bye, Connie."

"Love you."

"Love you too." I hung up and sat on a nearby bench. A freakin' blizzard was the last thing I needed, and I had no intention of holing up in that tiny apartment with Craig. It wouldn't be too bad to ride out the storm here at the arena, though. The fireplace in the lounge worked and though I usually didn't dare turn it on overnight in case I overslept, I could get away with it during a blizzard. No one would be here and I could hunker down in there until it was over.

I'd need food, though, especially if the electricity went out, so I made a list and then grabbed my backpack and headed out to my RAV4. I'd stop at the Twisted Tinsel Bar on my way back for a burger and so I could watch the weather channel on the TVs there. Then I'd decide what I was going to do next.

The only thing I knew for sure was that I wasn't calling Remy.

No way, no how.

Well, probably not.

CHAPTER TWENTY-ONE

Remy

I drove to my mother's house on autopilot, still reeling from last night's discovery about Noelle. How had I not noticed? I was so fucking pissed off at myself I barely remembered the drive to Vancouver.

Noelle lived at the arena.

That's why she was always so secretive and cagey about her life and where she lived.

She didn't have a home.

I wanted to smack myself for missing something so huge, but she'd done a good job keeping it a secret. No wonder she was so nervous about trusting anyone; she had very little left to lose and I guessed her pride was one of those things.

I didn't know what to do about it, though.

"Remy?" My mother's voice penetrated my dark thoughts and I looked up in surprise.

We were having dinner and Ashton was telling a funny story about his last hockey game, but I hadn't been listening.

"Do you want to talk?" she asked gently.

"About what?" Ashton asked curiously.

"I think something's happened with Noelle," Mom said.

"Who's Noelle?" Ashton asked, looking from Mom to me and back again.

"Someone I've been seeing," I said, taking a sip from my wine glass.

"Here?"

"In Garland Grove."

"What happened?"

"I'm stupid and she's stubborn," I muttered.

"That says a lot," Mom said, chuckling. "Would you like to elaborate?"

I blew out a breath. I hated to break Noelle's confidence but she hadn't confided in me. I'd found out on my own, and anyway, there was no one I trusted more than my mother and brothers. "She's...homeless. I didn't realize it until after we'd had our disagreement about spending Christmas together. I thought maybe if I followed her home from the arena, since she'd never invited me to her place, I might get some insight into what's going on. Instead, she never left the arena. I texted her, but before I could tell her I'd been waiting for her to come back out to her car, she lied and said she was going to bed."

"Except if she lives at the arena, she wasn't lying," Ashton pointed out.

"I guess not." I drummed my fingers on the table. "And now I don't know what the hell to do. Obviously, she didn't want me to know, but I'm crazy about her and the thought of her sleeping on the floor of the arena makes me insane."

"Does she have somewhere to go?" Mom asked worriedly.

"What do you mean?" I asked in confusion.

"There's a blizzard headed that way. We'll only get the tail end of it here, but up there in the mountains, it's going to be brutal. They're talking six feet of snow followed by ice. They're warning people to stock up on food and stay off the roads starting tonight."

"Are you sure?" I asked, yanking my phone out of my pocket. There was a strict no phone policy at the dinner table, but this was different.

"Pretty sure."

"Yeah, I saw something about it online too," Ashton said.

I pulled up a weather app and typed in Garland Grove. Sure enough, wintry conditions were coming, including a blizzard and maybe an ice storm as well. "Fuck," I muttered. "She could go to Connie's, but I don't know if she will. That situation is uncomfortable."

"You should call her," Ashton said, as if he knew anything about relationships. Hell, he might know more than I did at this point.

"Yeah. Excuse me." I got up and went into the other room, dialing Noelle's number. I had a feeling she wouldn't answer, and she didn't, so I left her a message.

"Hey, just wanted to check in because of the storm coming. Please be careful and call if you need anything, okay? I'd really like to talk, babe. I'm sorry we argued. I think we were both being a little stubborn. Will you call me back? Please?" I disconnected and went back to the dinner table. There was nothing else for me to do.

I watched the weather the next day with growing alarm. Noelle hadn't called me back and the storm was hitting Garland Grove hard based on what I saw on the news.

"Nothing from Noelle?" Mom asked, sinking down beside me.

I was in my father's old den, sitting in one of the chairs across from his desk because I never felt comfortable behind his desk. I missed the crotchety old bastard and was a little pissed off he'd died before we could work out our issues. I still had so many questions that would never be answered and that made it even worse.

"No," I said to my mother in response to her question. "She's stubborn."

"I know a few other people like that," she said softly.

"Who? Me and Dad?"

"And Kingston."

"Not Ashton?"

Ashton snorted out a laugh from the doorway where he'd been standing.

She smiled. "Ashton is my most easygoing child. You're my most driven. Kingston is the free spirit. The three of you are all so different, but I love how close you are. I hope you never lose that."

"I don't plan on it," I said. "Dad put a rift between us but I've fought to build it back for years. It's hard with us in three different places, but I think we're pretty close considering everything. Is Kingston going to make it for Christmas?"

"He said he'd be here on the twenty-fourth unless there are weather delays. His flight's supposed to land at two in the afternoon."

"I'll go get him," I said.

"You need to go get Noelle," she said gently.

I looked at her. "Mom, I don't know what to do. She obviously doesn't want to be with me."

"She doesn't want you to know how down and out she is. There's a difference."

"How do you know that? You met her for, like, two minutes."

"A woman recognizes another woman who's holding on to her pride by a thread. Believe me, I would know. Different circumstances, but I would have done anything to keep your father's infidelity a secret. It made me feel like a failure. As a wife, a mother, and a woman. Noelle is probably dealing with the same type of thing. I don't know what happened to her, but there was something in her eyes. The young woman I met seemed strong and independent, but extremely guarded, which means she cares about you."

"I love how women just know all this stuff," Ashton murmured, shaking his head. "I feel like I need to date older women."

"There's something to be said for older women," I told him.

"Can I see a picture of this woman you're screwing up with?" he asked.

"Uh, yeah." I pulled out my phone. We had a lot of pictures together for two people who hadn't known each other long. But my favorite was still the one of us in front of the tree, the night she'd complained she didn't have lipstick on.

"Oh, she's pretty," Ashton said, leaning over. "How old?"

"Twenty-seven."

"Well, if she dumps your sorry ass, can I have her?"

I playfully punched him. "Sorry, kid. This one is mine."

"Is she?" My mother arched one perfectly rounded brow. "Yours?"

Something twisted deep in my gut. I hadn't meant it in a misogynistic way; I was just crazy about her and unwilling to let her go without a fight.

"Go," Ashton said, making a shooing motion with his hands. "You know you want to."

"I don't know if I can get back up the mountain," I said, already getting to my feet.

"Take the snowmobile," Mom said.

Ashton and I both turned to look at her. "The what?"

Her cheeks actually turned pink, something I didn't think I'd ever seen happen to my mother. "Edward bought me one for my birthday. He likes to go snowmobiling and wanted me to be able to join him."

I had so many things to say to that, but I was too worried about Noelle. "You know what? We're going to have a talk about this Edward person," I said, "but not until I get back."

"It's on a trailer in the second garage," she said, ignoring what I'd said. "You can hitch it to my SUV and if the roads are bad, just leave the car in the nearest parking lot and take the snowmobile."

"Right. I need to change first."

"Don't forget to leave me the keys to your rental!" Ashton called. "So I have wheels while you're gone."

"Got it!" I ran upstairs to my room, pulling on the Under Armour I usually wore to work out, a long-sleeve thermal T-shirt, two pairs of sweats, and a hoodie. I had a waterproof winter jacket I'd wear on top of it, and that would have to be enough. I packed a small backpack I could wear on my back with a change of clothes, a toothbrush, deodorant, phone and charger, my wallet, and I'd grab protein bars and a few bottles of water before I left.

I had no idea what conditions I was going to find, but hopefully I wouldn't need the snowmobile.

"Be careful," Mom said, handing me three bottles of water and a few protein bars.

"You read my mind," I said, leaning over to kiss her cheek.

"Take these." She put some little packets into my hand. "They're hand and feet warmers. It gets cold on the snowmobile during non-blizzard conditions, so I imagine you'll be extra cold tonight."

"Here." Ashton handed me his ski mask. "This'll protect your face."

"Thank you. Both of you." I looked around. "I think I'm good."

"I hooked the trailer up to Mom's SUV while you were getting ready," Ashton said. "So you just have to hit the road."

"Please be careful," Mom said. "And for the love of everything holy, text or call to let me know you got there okay."

"Don't worry, I'm good." I squeezed her arm, lightly punched Ashton in the arm, and headed out to Mom's waiting vehicle.

Within forty-five minutes, the weather turned ugly. I was still a good distance from Garland Grove but there was no doubt I was going to need the snowmobile. I'd tried calling Noelle half a dozen times, but it always went straight to voicemail. Since I was pretty sure she hadn't turned off her phone just to avoid me, it made me nervous. Could cell towers be down in this weather? I'd heard of it happening for ice storms, but it was only snowing according to the weather updates.

I pulled off the road at a small diner and parked around back. The place was closed up tight, so I left a note on the inside of the windshield explaining that I'd had to park there because of the storm. I got the snowmobile down off the trailer and looked around. This was going to be a hell of a ride because I could barely see two feet in front of my face. How was I going to navigate the roads to get me to Garland Grove?

It was colder than a witch's tit, too. I rubbed my hands down my arms, grateful for Ashton's ski mask because my face would have been toast otherwise. Wearing two pairs of sweats had been handy too.

I sent a quick text to my mom telling her where I'd gotten off the highway and the name of the diner where I'd left her SUV. I was going to need the GPS on my phone to navigate so I put it in one of the zippered pockets in the front of my jacket and fired up the snowmobile. The GPS told me to go straight, in the direction I'd been driving, so I gunned the engine and took off in that direction.

Hang on, Noelle, I thought as I headed into the night. *I'm coming.*

CHAPTER TWENTY-TWO

Noelle

Preparing for the storm hadn't been too bad. I'd stocked up on a handful of snacks and groceries that wouldn't go bad, bought batteries, bottled water, and a thermal blanket I'd found on sale, and hunkered down at the arena in the family lounge. Everything had been going fine until the electricity went out. My phone was charged and I had a portable charger that was charged too, but I'd turned my phone off at that point so the battery would last as long as possible. I had a flash-light so I'd be able to see, but I'd thought the fireplace would still work without electricity and I'd been wrong.

Though the fireplace itself ran on gas, the pilot light wouldn't light without electricity, so it got cold inside a lot faster than I'd thought it would. I was wearing three layers of clothes, was wrapped in both the blanket and my sleeping bag, and I was still chilly. I didn't know what the temperature was, but the last time I'd looked outside, there had been whiteout conditions.

I should have sucked it up and gone to Connie's, or even knocked on Dwayne and Tandy's door, but my damn pride was going to get me killed one of these days. I truly hadn't thought it would be a big deal to ride out the storm here. Clearly, I'd miscalculated. We didn't get storms this bad very often, and never in December. Usually, if we got one, it was in January or February, deep in winter.

Shivering, I took off my jacket, put on another sweater, and then put the jacket back on. I'd been on the floor in front of the fireplace but since it wasn't any warmer, there was no reason to be on the floor. I was on the couch now, curled up with my blanket and sleeping bag, wondering if it was going to get any colder once it stopped snowing. I wasn't stupid, though, and once the weather cleared a little, I was going to walk to the Twisted Tinsel Bar and see if Horace was there. He lived in the apartment above the bar so he was usually around no matter how bad the weather was. He'd take me in without any questions.

Why was I so damn stubborn? If I'd just gone to Vancouver with Remy, none of this would be happening. I'd probably get my heart broken, but I already missed him so much it hurt, so what was the difference? At least I'd be warm and brokenhearted instead of a human popsicle.

What sane, rational person would choose to hunker down during a blizzard in an *ice arena*?

None.

Just a stubborn fool like me.

I had to go to the bathroom and the idea of stripping off any of my layers was daunting but peeing myself and sitting around in wet pants would be much worse. I took a deep breath and pulled free of the blanket and sleeping bag. I shivered in the cold air, but slid my feet into my sneakers, grabbed the flashlight and headed for the nearest bathroom.

It wasn't cold enough for me to freeze to death. At least, I was pretty sure it wasn't, especially not with the blanket and sleeping bag, but it was cold as hell. I never thought about the temperature inside the rink much because it was always chilly and I was used to it. This was a different level of cold and I really wanted to get out of here. Though I didn't have a lot of close friends, I knew almost everyone in town, and I had no doubt someone would welcome me in their home until the storm ended. The problem, of course, would be explaining why I couldn't hunker down at my own place.

Maybe waiting until June to find a place to live was too long. The plan had been to have money put aside for a rainy day before I looked for anything, so this wouldn't happen again, but I was tired of sleeping on floors and almost never having a hot meal. It was time for this crazy life of mine to go back to some semblance of normal, no matter how scary it was.

I came around the corner and something seemed off inside the lounge. I froze, my heart hammering against my ribs. Was that a shadow? Had someone come into the arena in the middle of a blizzard?

I'd never felt more stupid or alone or terrified than I did in that moment.

I turned and ran in the other direction just as a familiar voice yelled my name.

"Noelle! It's me—Remy."

I whirled around and ran straight to his arms, throwing myself against his chest and breathing in deeply.

"You scared me," I whispered.

"I'm sorry." He closed his arms around me tightly. "Where were you?"

"Bathroom."

"God, baby, it's freezing in here."

"I thought the fireplace would work but it didn't."

"Why didn't you call me?"

"I didn't think you wanted to talk to me."

"Even if I was mad, which I wasn't, I would have come if you'd called me. You know I wouldn't let anything happen to you."

"How did you get here?" I whispered against his chest, unwilling to move from the warmth of his embrace.

"Snowmobile."

I tipped up my head to see if he was kidding, but he looked serious. "Really?"

"Yeah. It's my mom's."

We didn't talk for a few seconds but he finally nudged me toward the lounge. "It's a little warmer in there," he said. "Let's go sit down."

"I'm so cold," I murmured, letting him pull me into his side on the couch. He wrapped the blanket and sleeping bag around us, and I settled back against his chest.

"Warming up a little?" he asked as he rubbed his hands up and down my arms.

"A little." I sighed. "How did you know I was here?"

"Gut feeling, I guess. I was worried about you and then when your phone started going straight to voicemail, I didn't know where you were or if you were safe. I know you've been living here, Noelle."

I groaned, burying my face in his shoulder. This was so damn embarrassing.

"Didn't you think you could trust me?" he asked, continuing when I didn't say anything. "Babe, talk to me."

"It's humiliating!" I whispered, horrified to feel tears sting my eyelids. "Someone as rich and successful as you dating a woman who didn't have enough in the bank for an emergency. Two back-to-back emergencies and one asshole roommate was all it took to put me on the street. And I'm so close to getting back on my feet..."

His arms tightened and he kissed the top of my head. "I'm so sorry. And I'm even sorrier you didn't think you could trust me."

"It wasn't about trust," I protested, looking into his handsome face. "It was about my pride."

"This blizzard is nuts," he said, his voice dropping. "You could have been holed up in here for days! And it's cold as balls. The temperature is supposed to drop another twenty degrees tonight after it stops snowing."

"I know."

"We need to get out of here."

"And go where?"

"I called Rudy and he said if we can get there, my old room is empty."

"That's almost five kilometers from here," I protested.

"Snowmobile," he said, grinning. "You game?"

"Electricity is out all over town, though."

"It is, but Rudy's place is heated with gas, and there's a fireplace, if nothing else."

"I would kill to be warm."

"I can think of a much less drastic measure." He slowly got to his feet and held out his hands. "Let me take care of you, Noelle. Until the storm is over. Then you can go right back to your life."

I took his hands and let him pull me to my feet, my eyes searching his face. Staring up at him, my pride, my embarrassment, everything dissolved as if it had never been there. He'd ridden a freakin' snowmobile to get to me. To make sure I was okay. My own mother hadn't worried about me, but this gorgeous man I'd known for three weeks risked his life to check on me. Even after we'd broken up. My heart skipped a beat as I leaned against him.

"What if I don't want to go back to my life?"

CHAPTER TWENTY-THREE

Remy

I stared at her a little too long, trying not to read into her words but doing it anyway. Was I falling in love or what? My emotions were a roller coaster of desire, frustration, and need. But this was neither the time nor the place for that kind of conversation. "Pack up what you'll need for a few days, let's get to the B&B, and once we're warm, we'll talk, okay?"

"Okay." She threaded her fingers with mine, squeezing for a second, before starting to gather up her things. She folded the blanket while I rolled up her sleeping bag and we grabbed her pillows, and a burlap bag that looked like it had water and snacks.

"Where's your stuff?"

"Most of it is in the women's locker room. I can grab my backpack and duffel bag and we'll be good to go."

"Great." We carried her things to the locker room and I held the flashlight while she rearranged her bag, put on her boots, and stuffed the sleeping bag and blanket into two lockers.

"First thing we're doing after this storm is over is buying you a winter coat," I grumbled. "And don't even think about saying no."

She didn't say anything but flashed me an impish little grin. I picked up her duffel with one hand and grabbed one of her hands with the other and we made our way to the back exit where I usually saw her go in and out. Her car was back there too, though it was currently almost completely covered with snow. I'd left the snowmobile there as well, and hopefully it would only take us a few minutes to get to the B&B.

When I woke in the morning, Noelle was still wrapped in my arms, fast asleep. I got out of bed slowly so as not to wake her, and used the bathroom. Peeking through the curtains, it looked like it had finally stopped snowing and there was a white blanket of snow covering everything. In the distance, I saw crews working on electric lines and a lone police vehicle cruising down the street. The sky was still gray and gloomy, but there were lights in the windows of other houses on the street, and there were a couple of people outside using blowers to free their vehicles from the snow.

I couldn't decide if I wanted to go back to bed, check my email, or go downstairs to find something to eat, but in the end, I slid beneath the sheets and wrapped my arms around Noelle again. I wasn't sure what we were doing or what was going to happen next, but the panic I'd felt when I'd thought she could be in trouble told me she was already too important to just walk away.

With me living in Florida and her here in BC, our choices were limited. Either we were going to end it completely, do the long-distance thing for a while, or get married. There really wasn't anything in between, and somehow, marriage didn't scare me anymore. Well, it had never scared me, but it had definitely given me pause considering my father's inability to keep it in his pants.

I wasn't him, though. From the outside looking in, it was probably crazy to be thinking this way after three weeks, but I'd never given a shit what other people thought. The only people's opinions who mattered in this instance were mine and hers. Of course, convincing Noelle to do anything was usually a lesson in futility but this was important enough to try.

"Do you think they have coffee downstairs?" she murmured sleepily.

"They might." I chuckled, kissing her forehead. "You want coffee?"

"So much."

"How about I run downstairs and see if I can get us some breakfast? I'll bring it up here or I'll have Rudy bring it up."

"You're the best." She smiled sleepily and for the first time possibly ever, I imagined what it would be like waking up next to the same woman every day. Those big green eyes. That silky blond hair. Those sweet pink lips. Yeah, I'd obviously lost my sanity, but it felt too good to overthink it. Since I couldn't explain what was going on with us, I pulled on a sweater and padded down the stairs. Rudy had just come in from the outside and was warming up by the fireplace.

"Just turned on the generator," he said. "Crews outside said we should have electricity again by midday so I'm going to leave it on a while. Vera's making waffles and bacon, and I figured we could all take quick showers, charge up phones and whatnot, and go from there."

"Sounds perfect," I replied. "Would it be all right if I took some coffee upstairs for Noelle and I until breakfast is ready?"

"No problem at all. In fact, Vera will bring up a couple of plates once it's ready." He paused. "How long you think you'll be here this time, Remy?"

"The morning of the twenty-fourth, I'm heading back to Vancouver." I paused. "Would you do me a favor, Rudy?"

"If I can."

"If Noelle decides not to come with me, will you let her stay here for a while? I'll pay you, but she can't know. She has to think you're just being nice."

Rudy nodded knowingly. "Stubborn as they come, that one. But she's a good girl. I hope you're treatin' her right. Now go get some coffee. Things will work out the way they're supposed to."

I wasn't sure what that meant, but I got two cups of coffee from Vera and went back upstairs. Noelle was just coming out of the bathroom and she looked stunning to me, even with no makeup and her hair back in a ponytail.

"Thank you." She took a cup from me and sighed happily as she had her first sip. "Best part of my day."

"Tell me about it." I sipped my own and sank into one of the chairs by the window. "Come sit with me, babe."

She turned, a smile playing on her lips. "Do you know, I don't think anyone has ever called me babe before?"

"Do you dislike it?"

"Not at all. I love it." She sank down in the other chair, holding the coffee mug with both hands.

"Are you ready to talk?" I asked gently.

"I guess so."

"I just want to help, to get to know you better and figure out where this thing between us is going."

"I know. It's just…embarrassing."

"Don't ever be embarrassed with me. I was born with a silver spoon in my mouth but I am acutely aware of how lucky I am. I don't hold it against anyone who wasn't born with what I was."

"Promise you won't think less of me?" Her eyes were filled with insecurity and pain. So much so that I tugged her out of her chair and onto my lap.

"Promise. Now tell me how you wound up living at the arena." I wrapped one arm around her waist and held my coffee with the hand of the other.

She looked away, chewing the inside of her cheek. "It started with a broken leg. I was working two jobs then. I did my thing at the arena part-time, but I also worked the front desk at a hotel in Whistler. The problem was that it was my right leg, and no matter how hard I tried, I couldn't drive. I was going to be out for six weeks and they fired me. Since I was only part-time, I didn't have any benefits. This was two years ago, and I had two roommates, so I figured I'd be okay. Money would be tight, but I could still hobble around at the arena. Except, I couldn't." She sighed, putting her coffee cup on the small table and resting her chin in her hand. "I fell on my crutches and broke my wrist."

"Oh, baby." I grimaced, imagining how frustrating that must have been.

"Dwayne and Tandy helped out as much as they could, so I wouldn't get fired from that job too, but then it was like the hits kept coming. The brakes went out on my car, which set me back a lot. Then I needed new tires. Like, they were completely bald, and I couldn't put it off any longer. Those two things wiped out my meager savings, and then, because I have no luck at all, my car insurance randomly went up. There were four or five more little things that all happened at once, and for the first time ever, I didn't have my share of the rent. My roommates were cool about it at first, but I had no money coming in and I still couldn't work."

"Did they kick you out?" I asked gently.

"When I couldn't come up with rent for the second month, they asked me to leave. I sold a bunch of my things and came up with enough money to move in with this woman I knew named Jasmine. She loves to party and was always out, so she said I could sleep on the pull-out couch in her living room for cheap. I told her I wouldn't have any money for a month, until the cast came off, and she was cool with it if I cleaned up a little around the apartment. I finally got the cast off my leg, so I could drive again, but no one was hiring. Jasmine wasn't home much, and she didn't care, so it worked out for both of us until she started bringing a creepy new guy home."

I put down my coffee and tightened my arms around her. She'd shuddered slightly and I wanted her to remember I was right here and not going anywhere.

"What happened?" I gently prompted her.

"He was always hitting on me, right in front of Jasmine, and it seemed like she was cool with watching, if you know what I mean. That's not my thing, so I kept telling him to leave me alone, but he was persistent. And with me on the couch, he had easy access to me. Then one night, things blew up. He wouldn't take no for an answer and literally attacked me. I hit him with the lamp on the side table and knocked him out cold."

"That's my girl." I gently kissed her temple.

"Yeah, well, Jasmine was hysterical, and she literally kicked me out then and there. Told me to pack my shit and leave. And of course, Connie had just had Daphne, so I couldn't impose on them. So I started sleeping at the arena. Dwayne figured it out, but I told him my roommate brings home weird men and that I just sleep at the arena on those nights. I think he knows better, but he doesn't say anything."

"He cares about you," I said gently. "Like a lot of people around here. Including me."

Those sparkling emerald eyes of hers lifted to meet mine. "And that's why I couldn't bear to tell any of you how close to rock bottom I've been. I'm almost there, almost out of the arena and ready to rent a room somewhere, but I promised myself I wouldn't until I had at least three months' worth of expenses in savings, in case something like that happened again. I refuse to be in a position where one broken leg could derail everything I've worked for."

"I'll never let anything happen to you, Noelle."

CHAPTER TWENTY-FOUR

Noelle

I wanted to protest, tell him I was okay, that I had everything under control. But that would have been a lie. I'd almost frozen to death because I was stubborn and proud and sometimes too much. Even for me. Human beings weren't meant to be solitary. We were social creatures at our core, even the most introverted of us, and we all needed help sometimes. Having friends, especially ones who cared enough to jump on a snowmobile in a blizzard, was important. And more than that, Remy was important.

"It's hard to ask for help," I said softly. "It's hard to admit you've failed at almost everything. I have a degree I can't use unless I move to a big city, which I can't do without money. I don't have the earning potential in a small town like Garland Grove to save up that kind of money, so it's a catch-22 and I hate everything about being in a position like this."

"But you're not alone," he said, taking one of my hands between both of his. "Isn't that what you've been telling Connie? That she can leave Craig because she's not alone? Well, she can count on you and you can count on me."

"Connie is literally the only person in my entire life I've been able to count on," I said, waves of emotion making my voice a little shaky. "We've only known each other three weeks, Remy."

"But sometimes you just know," he said.

"What do we know?"

"That there's something between us that I've never felt with anyone." He cupped the side of my face. "That I'm going to do absolutely everything I can so we can be together. That I don't want to lose you."

I nestled against him, my face buried in the side of his neck, holding on like I'd never held on to anyone before. No matter how many times my brain told me to be careful, my treacherous heart told me it was okay. Remy was the one. The one for what remained to be seen, but right now and for the foreseeable future? He was everything I'd ever dreamed of.

"You okay, babe?" His soft, gravelly voice made my insides clench with longing and my battered soul give in to what it wanted.

"I need you," I whispered.

"Breakfast will be here any minute," he whispered back. "Can you hang on until then?"

We laughed together, softly, our lips lightly touching.

The knock on the door made us jump but Remy got up, holding me in his arms, and gently put me on the bed before padding over to open the door.

"Thanks, Vera," he said. "Smells wonderful."

A moment later she was gone and he'd put the tray with our breakfast on the dresser. Before I could say anything, he stripped off his sweats and T-shirt and crawled under the covers.

"I believe you're wearing too many clothes," he said, giving me a look that made my insides quiver expectantly.

I wiggled out of the layers of clothes I'd been wearing and then crawled back under the covers next to Remy, our bodies close together. But instead of ravishing me the way he usually did, Remy just lay there, trailing the fingers of one hand along my hairline, my jaw, my collarbone.

"You're so beautiful," he murmured. "I love looking at you."

"I love the way you look at me," I admitted breathlessly. "No one's ever looked at me like they really see me."

"I can't see anyone else when you're in the room," he said, leaning in to kiss me. And again, the passion was there, but it simmered beneath the surface while his focus was on teasing and seducing me. As if I needed to be seduced. I was so far gone for this guy, all he had to do was look at me and I melted.

We kissed tenderly. Not rushing, not intensifying, just touching and exploring like it was the first time all over again. And it was wonderful.

"Do you trust me, Noelle?" His voice was barely a whisper against my ear and I couldn't help but hesitate.

"I'm trying," I whispered back.

"Are you protected against pregnancy?"

I nodded. "Yes, I have an IUD."

"Do you trust me to make love to you without a condom?"

"I...yes." There was no other answer because I knew he'd wear one if I said no, but I didn't want to say no. Not to this, not to anything. How could I trust him with my whole being if I didn't even trust him to be healthy and safe?

His eyes locked with mine and he slid into me without another word. His forehead dropped to mine and he didn't move.

"This is the best part," he said, nipping at my lips. "Just being inside you and enjoying the intimacy, before we lose control."

I sighed happily, my eyes fluttering closed because while maybe it wasn't the *best* part, it was definitely up there. "Mmhm."

"And now that I have your undivided attention, tell me what you want."

I forced my eyes open, trying to focus on his words instead of everything I was feeling. "Um...is this a trick question."

He shook his head, slowly pulling almost all the way out and then stopping.

"This isn't fair."

He chuckled. "Did I ever claim to play fair?"

"What do I want in what regard?" I asked when I realized he wasn't going to move until I answered his question.

"The thing you want most."

I gazed up at him as a million thoughts raced through my mind. But only one thing stood out; the only thing that mattered. "You."

He pushed back in with enough force to make us both grunt. "Don't say what I want to hear," he growled. "The truth."

"You."

He started to move again, slow and methodical, as if testing out every inch of me to see what made me squirm.

"A new place to live?" he panted. "A new car? What else?"

I shook my head, finding it a little hard to concentrate. "Just you."

"Aw, fuck, Noelle." His mouth fused to mine and everything blurred into a hazy cloud of ecstasy. His body, my body, our mingled breaths. I was helpless to do anything but go along for the ride.

. . .

With our bodies spent and our hearts still hammering, neither of us said anything for a long time. He'd rolled off of me and we were on our backs side by side, fingers laced between us.

"Come to Florida with me," he said after a while.

"I can't," I said sadly. "We never got the passport thing done."

"I'm going to get my attorney to handle it, okay? I'd mentioned it to him and there are services that will expedite it for us. Is that all right with you?"

I nodded. "Yes. Thank you."

"I don't know what it'll take to get a tourist or resident visa for you, but I'll have him work on that too. I think you can come for a few months before we have to worry about it."

"And then what?" I asked quietly. "I can't leave the arena for a few months and then just come back like I wasn't gone."

"I know." He turned onto his side. "You trust me, right?"

I looked into his eyes. "Didn't we already have this conversation?"

"Then I'm going to take care of everything. As soon as the shops open, we're going to go Christmas shopping and then we're heading back to Vancouver to spend time with my family."

I bit my lip. "Remy?"

"Yeah, babe?"

"I'd like to spend a little time with Connie. I think she's going to dump Craig after Christmas and I don't think they have anything to eat or gifts for the kids."

"Then we'll add Christmas-for-Connie-and-family to our shopping list."

Tears unexpectedly welled in my eyes and I swiped at them. "I keep wanting to say no, that it's too much."

"Listen to me." He gently gripped my chin between two of his fingers. "This isn't about making you or anyone else feel bad. Do you know how much money I donate to random charities every year? Tens of thousands. And none of it means anything other than tax write-offs and occasionally some good press. This? This is much more important because it's personal. I'm going to give every single employee at the rink a Christmas bonus of a thousand dollars. Because I can and because I want to. I'm going to give Connie and the kids and that fuckhead she's engaged to a Christmas they'll never forget. Not because of you, but because I feel good doing nice things for others. I'm going to give Rudy and Vera a gift card for enough gas to keep that generator running for a year. And if you know of anyone else in town who's hurting, who needs help but is too proud to ask for it, tell me who and I'll find a way to make their holidays and lives better too."

"How are you such a good guy?"

"I dunno." He cocked his head. "You look like you're going to cry. Does me being nice make you want to cry?"

I stared into his face, tears pouring down my cheeks, and realized I was in love with him. Three days, three weeks, or three years. The length of time we'd known each other didn't make any difference; I was completely gone for this guy. And since there were no words to adequately describe what I was feeling, I kissed him.

"You're a bit of a nympho, eh?" he teased when we finally pulled apart, playfully patting my backside.

"Apparently. But breakfast before any more of that!"

He just chuckled and climbed out of bed.

CHAPTER TWENTY-FIVE

Remy

We spent the rest of the day helping Rudy and Vera shovel and blow the snow both in front of their bed and breakfast and the rest of the street. From there, we headed to the arena to check on things and while we were making sure there were no leaks or anything else that needed attention, I called my attorney to talk to him about Noelle's passport situation.

"I'm glad you called," Dennis Curry said when he answered. "Guy named Ryder Long left a message. Says he's interested in the Garland Grove Ice Arena."

"What?" I was shocked. I'd had no idea someone would not only want to buy it but was reaching out to me before I even put it up for sale. "How did he know it's for sale?"

"No idea. Told him we'd get back to him after Christmas." Dennis paused. "You are going to sell it, right?"

I sighed. "I don't know yet. Give me a few days."

"What's up with you?" he demanded. "You were supposed to be there two days. And now you've been there almost a month."

"Long story," I said. "But that passport thing I mentioned the other day? I need you to get on it. I need one for her ASAP."

Dennis chuckled. "Jesus Christ. I thought it was a myth."

"What?" I grunted, though I had an idea what he meant.

"This is about a woman. You skated on that damn rink and fell in love or lust or something."

"I pay you to take care of shit for me," I muttered. "Not to give me shit."

He laughed. "I can't wait to meet her. I'll send you some paperwork that she'll need to fill out and take care of the passport."

"And as soon as possible, we need to work on getting her a visa so she can stay in Florida with me."

Dennis burst out laughing. "Oh, now I really can't wait to meet this woman."

"I swear to God, I'm going to fire your ass."

"You've said that at least a dozen times in the decade we've been working together."

"I'm not kidding," I growled, though I had no intention of firing him. Dennis was one of the people I trusted most in the world, and I knew from experience how hard it was to find people like him.

"Okay, settle down. Let me find out what's what and I'll call you back, okay?"

"Thanks. I also need you to order a few things for me and have them shipped to my mother's house in Vancouver." I gave him a list of what I wanted.

"Anything else?" he asked.

"I'll let you know. And thanks."

"Talk to you later."

I disconnected and took a deep breath. Why did the ribbing about Noelle bother me so much?

I already knew the answer, of course. I was falling in love and didn't want anyone to make fun of that. Even in jest.

"Hey, are you ready to go?" Noelle came around the corner.

"Yup. I was just talking to my lawyer about your passport. He doesn't think it'll be a problem to get it by New Year's Eve so we can head to Florida."

"Oh, wow. I didn't think it would be that fast."

"I'm sure he has it under control."

"I made a few calls and found out that most of the shops are staying open late so people can get their shopping done since everything was closed for two days."

"Perfect. You ready to do some Christmas shopping?"

"Yes."

. . .

We started at the toy store. I bought Alexander a bike, some superhero figurines, and a bunch of coloring books, crayons, and regular books. We got more practical things for Daphne, including a swing so Connie didn't have to hold her all the time and some developmental toys that would keep her busy while also helping her learn. From there we headed to a clothing store where we stocked up on things for both kids, as well as for Connie. I wasn't going to buy anything for Craig since Connie was kicking him to the curb anyway, but we were also going to the grocery store tomorrow to buy them enough food to last a few weeks, as well as a feast for Christmas.

We made a few more stops, buying wrapping paper rolls and tape and bows since we didn't have any of that stuff, and we sat up until almost three in the morning wrapping presents and talking. I'd never been in this kind of relationship, where being together around the holidays not only felt natural but was also the most fun I'd had outside of hockey.

I'd paid careful attention to everything Noelle looked at and touched, making mental notes and then leaving requests for the store owners to put certain things aside for me so I could pick them up tomorrow. I was going to surprise Noelle for Christmas whether she wanted me to or not, but I had a feeling she was coming around. Her experience during the blizzard had changed her view of things. Or at least how she viewed me, and I was good with that.

I harbored no illusions that this thing between us had anything to do with magic, but whenever we were together, I felt like I was under a spell. Whether it was the idyllic small town, the holiday season that reminded me of being here as a kid, the woman herself, or some crazy combination of all of the above, I was already comfortable with the emotion I'd begun to feel. It made no sense, but things in my life rarely did, so I'd learned to go with it.

Now that Noelle had finally opened up to me and I was aware of her background, everything between us had become effortless. It seemed like my wealth still made her a little uncomfortable, but she was getting better about it. Seeing the look on Connie's face when we'd shown up with gifts and groceries had been enough to change Noelle's outlook, and we'd talked about it in the car after we'd left.

"I can't remember the last time I saw Connie so happy," she said. "Thank you for what you did for them today."

"It was my pleasure," I told her. "And I have another idea to help Connie too, but it depends on you."

"On me?" She looked over at me in surprise.

"If you want to be with me in Florida."

"I...I mean, I do, but what does that have to do with Connie?"

"I've been looking over everything about the arena and it desperately needs a manager. Someone to keep up with scheduling, turn in accurate numbers for payroll, make sure the concession stand is correctly staffed, stuff like that. I can make it a full-time job with benefits, and she can have the baby with her when she has to."

"This means you're assuming I'm not coming back," she said after a moment.

I reached for her hand. "I don't want you to come back. I want you with me."

"And if it doesn't work out between us?"

"I don't believe that will be the case."

"Remy. We have to be realistic. Especially me."

"If by some chance it doesn't work out, I'll make sure you get settled wherever you want, whether it's back in Garland Grove or Vancouver or somewhere else."

She swallowed. "Okay."

I glanced at her suspiciously. "That's it? Just okay?"

"I can't fight you anymore, Remy. I feel like I'm under some kind of spell when it comes to you and I'm helpless to resist, no matter what it is."

I parked in the circular driveway in front of my mother's house and turned to her. "Then we're under the same spell because I feel the same way."

"Then I guess there's nothing else to do except Christmas with your family." Her eyes met mine. "Do I look okay? I want to make a good impression on your mom."

I shook my head. "You look perfect, and I promise, my family is going to love you. Especially Kingston."

"Why Kingston?" Now she was the one who was suspicious.

I just laughed as I got out of the SUV. "You'll see."

I walked to the back of the vehicle and got out my big suitcase and the small one I'd bought for Noelle since her duffel was falling apart. I guided my wheeled suitcase toward the front steps with one hand and grabbed her hand with the other. Just as Kingston opened the door, grinning.

"Merry Christmas!" he called.

"Merry Christmas." I let go of Noelle's hand and ran up the steps, hugging him tightly.

"I knew it!" he whispered, laughing heartily. "I knew you were going to find someone at that rink and I was going to win the bet!"

"We're not married, asshole."

"Not yet!" Kingston pulled away and ran down the steps to greet Noelle. "Hi. I'm Kingston Knight, the older of Remy's two younger brothers."

Noelle was smiling at him, obviously taking in the visible neck tattoos, his nose ring, and some crazy black and blue hair that was new; his hair was naturally blond

"Nice to meet you." She smiled warmly. "I'm sorry if I'm staring. You just look so familiar."

"You didn't tell her?" Kingston spun around to me, shaking his head. "Dude."

"What didn't you tell me?" Noelle called, playfully tapping her foot. "Why do I feel like I know your brother?"

"Should I tell her?" I asked Kingston. "You know what, why don't you do it while you get the other bag and I go find Mom." I walked into the house and left Kingston with Noelle. She was a fan of Onyx Knight's music, and when she'd mentioned it, I'd decided not to tell her Kingston was my brother so it would be a surprise when she met him.

Sure enough, the squeal came a few seconds later and Mom arched a brow as I walked into the kitchen where she was mixing something in a bowl and Ashton was putting silicon baking liners on trays.

"Merry Christmas!" I called out, leaning over to kiss Mom's cheek and patting Ashton on the back.

"You didn't warn her about Kingston?" Ashton asked, laughing.

"Thought it would be more fun this way," I said.

"I'm leaving you," Noelle announced as she and Kingston came into the kitchen. He had an arm around her shoulders, and she was giving me the stink eye.

"I figured," I said, chuckling. "All my girlfriends leave me for him, the good-looking bastard." I wasn't in the least bit worried about my brother making moves on Noelle; he was just playing it up and being flirtatious because of our stupid bet.

"Hello, Noelle." Mom intervened, smiling at her. "Nice to see you again. Merry Christmas."

"Merry Christmas." Noelle smiled back.

"Babe." I reached for her hand. "This is my youngest brother, Ashton. Ash, this is Noelle Burrier."

"Hey, how's it going?" Ashton gave her a friendly grin.

"I feel like hot chocolate," Kingston said, rummaging in the fridge and pulling out the milk.

"Chocolate's in the cupboard," Mom told him.

Ten minutes later, Mom had two batches of cookies in the oven and we were settled around the island sipping hot chocolate.

"When are you heading to Florida?" Kingston asked me.

"Probably on the first. I have a full day of meetings on the second."

"Are you going with him?" Kingston asked Noelle.

She smiled. "We're waiting for my passport to come, but supposedly it's been expedited so my fingers are crossed."

"If not, she'll fly out as soon as she gets it," I said.

"When's the wedding?" Kingston asked, his eyes twinkling with mirth.

I kicked his foot. "Shut up," I muttered.

"When do you head out?" Ashton quickly redirected Kingston after catching my murderous glare.

"Twenty-eighth," he said. "We play in Jersey on the twenty-ninth, Madison Square Garden on the thirtieth." He looked at me. "You guys should come. It's going to be a great show."

"Passport," Noelle reminded him.

He grimaced. "Right. Forgot. Well, maybe it'll get here in time."

"How's hockey season going?" Noelle asked Ashton.

And that was it. Once we went down a hockey rabbit hole, Noelle was pretty much part of the family.

"Kingston, I had a thought," I told him. "You want to sing the national anthems at the Knights' first home game? I don't have the schedule yet, so I don't know if it'll be the US anthem only or both US and Canada." They would only do the Canadian anthem if the Knights were playing a Canadian team.

"Fuck yeah. That'll be October, right?" Kingston pulled out his phone. "We don't have tour dates or anything but as soon as you know, I can block off the time. This tour ends at the end of June and I think we're taking a break after that. We've been promoting the current album for more than two years. It's time to chill, go on vacation and record new music."

The five of us sat up late, talking, eating cookies, and giving my family the opportunity to get to know Noelle. She fit right in, talking shit about the current hockey season with Ashton and my mom, listening to Kingston's stories about life on the road, and conferring with my mother on what time to put the turkey in. We didn't get to bed until almost three in the morning, but it had been a great night. In fact, the best Christmas Eve I'd had in a long time, even though we'd gotten here late.

"Merry Christmas," she whispered as we dozed off.

"Merry Christmas, babe."

CHAPTER TWENTY-SIX

Noelle

It had been years since I'd gotten Christmas presents. Usually, Connie and I took whatever spare money we had and tried to do something together, like a girls' day out with lunch and window-shopping. So I hadn't been expecting anything on Christmas morning, much less the stack of packages that had my name on them.

"Remy!" I gave him a look. "What did you do?"

He shrugged. "I didn't do anything. I guess Santa came."

"I don't have anything for anyone!" she whispered. "I thought we were keeping it simple."

"This *is* simple. If I'd bought you a new car, like I wanted to, that would've been over the top. Don't you think?" His eyes twinkled and I didn't know whether to laugh or cry. But it was Christmas, and his family was watching, so I had no choice but to be gracious. Well, there were always choices, but as I'd told him last night, I was helpless to refuse him anything, especially when it came in brightly wrapped packages.

One of them was long and stick-shaped, and I gave him a look. "Is that what I think it is?"

He laughed. "You'll have to open it and see. I don't know what Santa had up his sleeve."

Deciding I was going to enjoy this, I dug into the gifts, and sure enough, he'd gone way overboard on the things he'd bought me, but I loved every single one of them. Especially my new set of hockey equipment and an amazing winter coat. There was also a limited-edition inaugural season Lauderdale Knights jersey—which wasn't even available to the public yet—and hockey skates. There was a theme to most of his gifts, but the whole family had gotten the limited-edition jerseys and Kingston said he would wear his when he sang the anthem next fall.

I excused myself to get another cup of coffee after I'd opened all my gifts and took a minute to catch my breath. Christmas this year was too much and everything I'd ever dreamed of all wrapped up in one dark-haired, bearded, retired hockey player. I'd never imagined having feelings this strong for someone I'd known less than a month, but here we were. And I'd agreed to move to another country to be with him.

It was overwhelming but in a good way. For whatever reason, I trusted Remy, and more than that, I trusted us as a couple. I kept trying to rationalize it, but in the end, there was no explanation for falling in love this quickly. And frankly, I didn't care anymore. I still had the money I'd been putting away for nearly a year, and I knew in my heart of hearts Remy wouldn't let anything happen to me, even if things didn't work out for us romantically. It was just the type of man he was.

"Are you all right, Noelle?" Aletha came in behind me, checking on something in the oven. "You looked a little overwhelmed by my son's generosity."

"I haven't gotten a single Christmas present since I was about thirteen," I admitted. "So yes, Remy's generosity is a little overwhelming. But he's such a great guy, it's hard to say no to him, and I don't really want to."

She smiled. "He's generous to a fault. Always has been. I didn't have the best marriage, but I got the three best sons in the whole world out of it, so it wasn't all bad."

"Your sons seem wonderful," I said, taking a sip of my fresh cup of coffee.

"I know this is all happening very quickly with you and Remy," Aletha said, taking a casserole out of the oven. "But you can be sure Remy will be there for you. No matter what."

"I feel that way too."

"Love each other," she said softly. "Communicate, and more than anything else, take care of each other emotionally. That's something that was missing in my marriage, so that's my advice to you, woman to woman. Don't let him get caught up in work—it's in the DNA of the Knight men to be workaholics—no matter how important he says it is. Don't ever let him put you second. And if he tries, put your foot down. I never did and it's my biggest regret. Anyway, enough of that." She put her oven mitt down and looked around. "I think it's time for breakfast. Will you help me take everything to the formal dining room?"

"Of course."

Her words echoed in my thoughts as I carried the casserole out to the dining room.

Love each other and communicate.

That seemed overly simple.

Maybe it was.

It rang true, though. Secrets caused nothing but trouble and I didn't have anymore. And it was so freeing.

Saying goodbye to Remy's family was harder than I'd thought it would be. I'd only known them a few days but I already adored all of them. Aletha was smart, educated, and a warm, loving matriarch. Kingston was extremely good-looking and even more talented; having him play piano and sing Christmas carols on Christmas Day was one of my favorite memories ever. And though young, Ashton was funny, sweet and also going to be a hottie when he got a little older. There was no doubt they all loved each other deeply and had accepted me into the fold without hesitation. The brothers teased and joked nonstop, and it had only taken a day before Kingston and I ganged up on Remy and Ashton or Aletha and I ganged up on all three guys.

There had never been so much love or laughter in my house growing up and my eyes had filled with tears when Kingston hugged me good-bye, since we'd had to leave the day after Christmas.

"Keep him on his toes," he'd whispered to me.

"Always."

"I don't know what you're saying over there," Remy yelled, "but stop talking shit about me!"

Kingston flipped him off before hugging his older brother. Then we'd hit the road back to Garland Grove. I'd forgotten about coaching the kids' hockey camp and I couldn't blow it off. I didn't need the money now that I was going to Florida with Remy, but there was no one else and those kids would all be let down if I didn't show up. Best of all, Remy was going to coach with me, which would be a huge surprise for the kids.

"Hey, listen to this," Remy said as we settled into our room at Rudy and Vera's B&B. "My attorney left me a message that two people are interested in the arena. I haven't even put it up for sale yet!"

"I don't want you to sell it," I said softly.

"Babe, I'm not going to have time to breathe the next six months.

Any free time I have will be devoted to you, so if things start going wrong here, I can't just drop everything to deal with them."

"Aren't you hiring Connie to manage the place?" I asked. "And, once we get my visa sorted out, I can fly back and forth to take care of things if that happens."

"Maybe one of them would want to be partners," he said thoughtfully. "Then we could share responsibilities. That would make it easier for us and I'm not worried about making money."

"Please make sure they can't sell it, that both of you need to agree before you sell it."

He leaned over to kiss my forehead. "If you don't want me to sell the arena, I won't."

"Thank you."

His phone rang and he made a face. "That's my attorney. I should take this. Hey, Dennis, what's up..." He seemed to be listening for a long time, his eyes moving to me and then looking away again. "Uh huh. Yeah. I'm gonna have to get back to you, okay? Yeah, thanks."

"What's wrong?" I asked automatically.

"Nothing's wrong, per se." He hesitated. "It's just, well, the visa thing is complicated."

My heart sank.

"So I won't be able to stay more than a few weeks?"

"If we just head to Florida next week, like we've planned, you can't stay more than a couple of months." His eyes met mine.

"Is there a but?" I asked.

"Kinda." He scratched his chin. "Jesus, this is *so* not how I pictured this moment."

"This moment?" I wrinkled my nose. "What's wrong?"

"Nothing's wrong, I just..." His voice trailed off and he stared into my eyes as he reached for my hands. He pulled me against him and wrapped his arms around me. "We wouldn't have to worry about it if we get married."

"M-married?" I was probably gaping at him, but I was completely floored. "It's been less than a month."

"I know." His eyes hadn't left mine. "But I don't want to be without you for any length of time and the only way I can keep you with me, no matter where I go or what I do, is if we're married."

"And...you want to?"

"Call me crazy, but yes." There was the tiniest flicker of uncertainty in his eyes. "I'll make you happy, Noelle. We'll have a good life. I want this. I know it's fucking crazy but I want you."

"If I say yes, there has to be a prenup."

"Okay."

"And I don't want a big wedding. Just you and me, at the outdoor rink. New Year's Eve."

I nearly choked. "What?"

"New Year's Eve is my favorite holiday, the rink is where we met, and the outdoor rink is the most romantic place in Garland Grove."

"Did Kingston put you up to this?" he demanded, though there was a smile on his face.

"Kingston?" I was so confused. "What are you talking about?"

"Never mind. Just an inside joke with Kingston and I...but seriously, will you marry me, Noelle?"

"Yes." I closed my eyes as he kissed me, our bodies moving together naturally, as if we'd been doing this much longer than a month.

"I don't think there's a waiting period here," he said.

"No. We just have to get the license."

"Do you have a minister you'd like to perform the ceremony?"

I shook my head. "I'm not religious, so anyone you find is okay with me."

"My mother and brother will have to be invited," he said. "And while I don't think Kingston can come back, he might if I charter a plane from New York."

"And Connie and the kids."

"Rudy and Vera."

"Dwayne and Tandy."

"Horace." We said the bartender's name together and burst out laughing.

"Oh my god." I remembered something. "Horace is an ordained minister. I don't know the details, but he performed the ceremony for a gay couple that frequents his bar so let's have him marry us! The Twisted Tinsel Bar was our first date, right?"

He chuckled. "It was and if he can marry us, that works for me."

"Oh my god." I threw myself at him all over again. "Are we really doing this?"

"Yes." He kissed the top of my head. "But before we do anything else, I have to tell you something."

"Okay." I looked up curiously.

"I don't want to say the words yet."

"What words?"

"The L-word." He brushed his fingers across my cheek. "We're rushing into everything, so let's hold out on that until the time is right. Something romantic and private and just for us. I couldn't surprise you with a ring or an engagement or even a wedding, but I'd like the first time I say those words to you to be the most personal, romantic, and wonderful moment in time we could ever imagine."

I tried to blink away my tears but they fell anyway. "You are truly the most amazing man I've ever met."

"And you're the most amazing woman I've ever met." He rested his forehead against mine. "So...you still want kids, right? Because if not, that's okay, but you have to be the one to tell my mother."

I laughed. "I do want kids. Not quite yet, but yes."

"Are you going to be comfortable hosting big team parties in Florida?"

"With you at my side, I'll be comfortable doing anything and everything."

"Who should we tell first?" he asked, pulling me close again.

"Your mom. Then Connie."

"Then we talk to Horace."

"And Kingston."

"We have a lot to do in the next few days."

"But there's only one thing I want to do right now." I pulled my top over my head.

Remy's eyes darkened. "That makes two of us."

————

"I now pronounce you...man and wife!" Horace grinned at us. "You may kiss your bride."

We were on the outdoor ice rink of the arena surrounded by a handful of the people closest to us. Kingston had arrived an hour before the ceremony and was taking a red-eye back to the east coast late tonight. He stood up for Remy and Connie stood up for me. Horace had kept the ceremony short and to the point, and when we kissed, everyone clapped.

Everyone in attendance was on skates, except Daphne, whom Ashton was holding since she'd taken a liking to him, and the moment we kissed we were immediately surrounded by everyone as they wished us good luck.

"Instead of a first dance, how about a first skate?" Dwayne suggested. "Pick a song, any song, and I'll get it on the speakers."

"Would you indulge me?" Remy asked me.

"Of course."

"The Beatles' 'Here, There and Everywhere,'" he said softly.

"I love that song," I whispered.

"And I love you."

We both froze, our eyes locked.

"I..." He seemed at a loss for words, as if he hadn't planned to say it.

"I love you too," I said softly. "Pick me up." I reached up and he grabbed me by the waist, lifting me so I could wrap my legs around his waist. "It's been on the tip of my tongue all day, and as usual, you beat me to it. I love you, Remy Knight. And this was the absolute most romantic time to say it."

He crashed his mouth to mine and I heard Kingston yelling, "We play in Fort Lauderdale in March, big brother!"

I felt my new husband groan.

"What's that about?" I asked, chuckling.

"I'll tell you later." Then he kissed me again. And again.

EPILOGUE

Remy
One Year Later

It had been almost a year since the last time I'd been to Garland Grove. Noelle had been back and forth, keeping an eye on the arena and helping Connie get settled in her new life. Connie had broken up with Craig and moved into a small town house a few minutes from the rink, and from what Noelle told me, her life was a thousand times better than it had been.

It was Christmas Day and we'd driven in from Vancouver, including my mother and brothers. We had to get back to Fort Lauderdale by the thirtieth, so I'd arranged to meet up with the other owners of the arena, who'd also planned to be in town for the holidays. It would also allow me to give Noelle her final Christmas present in what I hoped was a romantic, thoughtful way. We'd spoiled each other for our first Christmas as a married couple, but I loved doing it and she was getting more and more comfortable with letting me.

Life was better than I'd imagined it would be and Noelle was everything I'd hoped a life partner could be. She loved everything about her new life as far as I could tell, from our intracoastal mansion to the hockey team that meant so much to me to my family. She talked to my mother more than I did, and Kingston adored her, which was kind of cool because he didn't like many people in general.

"Hey, Remy! Hi, Noelle!" Holly Turner waved at us and we waved back as Noelle and I finished lacing up our skates.

"You guys are early!" Noelle called to her, referring to her and her husband Forest. "Wait for me!" She got up and skated onto the ice, hugging Holly as they two of them skated off, whispering to each other.

"How the hell does she do it?" I mused aloud.

"How does Noelle do what?" Jacques Frontier sank down beside me and kicked off his boots as he started putting on his skates. He was now in charge of the hockey program at the rink and striving to make it one of the elite programs in the province. He'd already brought in a few more retired pros to assist with coaching.

"Make friends with everyone, even long distance. She and Holly have only met once before but they're fast friends."

"You know how women are—they bond. Not like us crusty old codgers."

"Speak for yourself!" I laughed, getting to my feet. "Where's Serenity?"

Jacques shrugged, though he was grinning. "She was right behind me but she probably stopped to talk to everyone."

"I'm familiar with that concept. See you out there!" I skated off in search of my wife and found her huddled with Holly, Amy, and Serenity. They were giggling like teenagers, and I couldn't help but smile. Nothing made me happier than seeing Noelle happy, but seeing her here on the ice where we'd gotten married was extra special. Especially with the surprise I had for her.

"Hey, babe." I smiled at the four ladies. "Would you guys mind if I stole my wife for a few minutes?"

Amy winked since she, Holly, and Serenity knew about my surprise. "Go have fun, you two."

"What are we doing?" Noelle asked, looking up at me curiously.

"I have one more Christmas present for you," I said, taking her hand as we glided around the ice.

"A diamond-crusted butt plug?" she asked, blinking innocently. "Oh, wait, no...it's a gold-plated vibrator."

I chuckled. "Someone must be horny. But no, smartass, it's neither of those things. I'll keep those ideas in mind for your birthday, though."

She rolled her eyes, playfully nudging me. "What is it? Because I have one more present for you too."

I pulled an envelope out of the inside pocket of my coat. "Merry Christmas, babe."

She slowed down as she took it from me and opened it. Her eyes widened and then flew up to meet mine. "Remy! You can't...I mean, why..." Her voice failed altogether, and she turned, throwing herself in my arms. "Oh, god, I love you so much."

"I love you too, baby." I kissed the top of her head.

"But why would you give me your share of the arena?" she whispered. "You've already given me so much and..."

"Because I don't care about it the way you do, and I wanted you to have something that was yours. I mean, you still share it with Ryder, Forest, and Jock, but it felt like a boys' club so I thought maybe they needed a woman to keep them in line."

She smiled. "I'm not going to have time to run an arena."

"You've made the time to come out here every other month for the last year," I protested. "What's going to change now that you're part owner?"

She reached into her coat and pulled out what looked like a picture. "This is what's going to change. Sometime in July."

I blinked in confusion.

It was an ultrasound photo.

"Babe, what..." Reality dawned and my mouth might have fallen open but I couldn't be sure because I'd scooped her up and was spinning her around. "We're having a baby?! You're pregnant. Holy shit, I'm going to be a dad!"

"Surprise." She was laughing, her legs wrapped around my waist.

I kissed her as tenderly as I knew how, holding her tightly and imagining what it was going to be like to see her carrying our child. I loved this woman more than life itself. It may have been a cliché, but I meant every word of it.

"This is the best gift ever," I said when we finally came up for air.

"Your mother is going to be so excited," she whispered.

"I'm so excited." I gently set her on her feet. "So...is it a secret?"

"Not anymore."

"I can tell people?"

"Of course."

I turned and waved to our friends, pulling her along with me as we approached them. "We're pregnant!" I announced.

"Right on!" Jock high-fived me.

"Congratulations!" We were immediately surrounded by a group of people I hadn't even known a year ago. Hell, I barely knew them now, but they'd become family over the last year, albeit long-distance.

Ryder Long had contacted me first, willing to buy me out, but Noelle hadn't been happy about it so I'd put him off a few days. Then I'd heard from a movie star named Holly Turner, who'd also wanted to buy it. And finally, Jacques had thrown his hat in the ring, and I'd had to make a decision. I truly didn't have the time to run things, and I'd known Noelle and I would have a full, busy life in Fort Lauderdale.

Ironically, it had been Noelle's idea to let the three of them buy into it and the four of us had met via videoconference to talk it out. Everyone had been amenable, and our lawyers had drawn up the papers. When I'd gotten the idea to give Noelle my share as a Christmas present this year, I'd discussed it with my co-owners, and none of them had a problem with it, so I'd drawn up the papers.

We'd come up with the plan to meet up here in Garland Grove on Christmas Day to celebrate how we'd all essentially fallen in love here a year ago, and it felt like they were old friends now, instead of people I barely knew.

"I say we do this every year," I said solemnly.

"I no longer work holidays," Holly said. "I wouldn't miss being in Garland Grove for Christmas." Her gaze slid to the children she'd officially adopted with Forest and lowered her voice. "Especially not now when the children still believe in Santa." She squealed as Forest skated up to pull her against his side. "This one might still believe too, so there's that."

"If you're talking about Santa, then the answer's yes," Forest said. "Did you tell them our news?"

She poked him in the ribs. "You're not supposed to tell anyone yet."

He grinned and placed his hand over Holly's belly. "But I'm so excited and these guys are practically family."

"We're having a baby," Holly said. "And it's way too early to talk about it but my husband's terrible at keeping secrets." She turned to Amy. "Enough about us. What about you two? Can you come for Christmas next year?"

"It's not too far for us," Amy replied, smiling. "So we'll be here barring any unforeseen circumstances. Ryder is now a believer in taking vacations." She caught her boyfriend's eye and grinned "Although the break in the hockey schedule at Christmas is usually pretty short. But we'll make it work!"

"Us too." Jacques nodded.

"Hot chocolate anyone?" Connie skated up to us with a tray containing eight cups of hot chocolate.

"Thank you!"

Everyone got a cup and I lifted my glass. "Merry Christmas, everyone."

"To extended family," Amy said, winking at Noelle.

"To friendship," Holly said, nodding.

"To us," Jacques agreed.

"To the Garland Grove Ice Arena," Noelle said softly.

We pressed our glasses together.

"Until next year."

Thank you so much for reading Knight Before Christmas.
Next up is the Lauderdale Knights series! You can flip the page to read
the first chapter from SLAP SHOT, which is the first book in the series
—where you'll see more of Remy and Noelle!

EXCERPT FROM "SLAP SHOT"

Chapter One
Julliet

I glanced at the time on my phone half a dozen times as I waited for traffic to let up. I was beyond excited to be attending the inaugural season opener for the new professional hockey team here in my hometown of Ft. Lauderdale, but I'd been late leaving work and now I was going to miss the warm-up. Two of my brothers, Mario and Tony, who also worked at our family pizzeria, had left early, of course, leaving me to handle all the last-minute details to make sure the staff was ready for the dinner shift.

I loved my big, loud Italian family, but they drove me crazy sometimes.

Traffic finally moved, I found a parking spot, and hurried through the lot to the entrance. We'd bought four season tickets, and though there were technically nine of us who'd shared in the cost, I'd paid a quarter of it myself, so I had a seat at every game if I wanted it. Which I did. I loved hockey and getting a team here in South Florida was the most exciting thing to happen to me in a long time. Hopefully, hockey games would make up for my disaster of a personal life. But I wasn't thinking about that tonight.

I grabbed a glass of wine and a bag of popcorn and finally found our seats. Mario, Tony, and Tony's wife Desi were already in the seats and they looked up as I sat down.

"You're late," Desi said, grinning at me.

I rolled my eyes. "Apparently, I'm the only one who cares about whether or not the dinner shift is prepared."

Tony turned to me, eyes wide as if he had no idea what I was talking about, but there was a grin playing on his lips. "What'd we forget to do?"

"Oh, I don't know…count out the register from the day shift cashier? Make sure everyone on the schedule showed up so we wouldn't leave them short with no manager on duty. Shit like that?"

Mario grimaced but Tony just laughed. "That's why we have you. We cook, you do business stuff."

"Sorry, sis," Mario said softly. "We were just excited."

"Because I'm not excited?" I met his gaze squarely. This wasn't the first time they'd cut out early and left me working late to handle things that weren't necessarily my job. It was a family business, but I worked more hours than all of them.

"Are you actually mad?" Tony looked confused.

"I missed the warm-up," I said, trying not to snap at him. "That's my favorite thing. This was the very first one. *And I missed it*. There will never be another first game or first warm-up."

Tony blew out a breath. "I'm sorry," he said. "Honest to god, it never occurred to me we were leaving you with a lot to do."

"Because all you pay attention to is the food and your paycheck," I responded. "You don't care about the business side and I can't do it all. In fact, going forward, I'm not going to do it all. You guys are going to step up, or I'll find another job."

The three of them stared at me as if I'd just sprouted a unicorn horn.

"You can't leave the pizzeria," Mario said.

"Jules, you're not serious." Even Desi was gaping at me.

"I absolutely am. This is the last time I miss something important to me because you guys think you can cut out whenever you feel like it. I worked until midnight last Wednesday because Edie forgot to input the timecards. If it hadn't gotten done, our staff wouldn't have gotten paid on Friday. But you guys were out the door at four-thirty like your asses were on fire. You knew there was something up with the time-cards, but you just assumed I'd handle it. This is the last time."

"That's my bad," Desi said. "I should have stayed with you but Tony said…" She reached over and punched his arm. "You told me it was no big deal, that Jules would handle it in a few minutes!"

"I didn't know nothing had been input," he said, rubbing his arm. "I thought it was a computer glitch and I don't do so good with technology, so I figured Jules had it covered."

I took a sip of wine and stared out at the ice. I hadn't meant to bring this up at the game, but I was pissed about missing the warm-ups. It might have been a little petty, but I had a lot going on in my life and my brothers often treated me like a cute pet who needed feeding and the occasional petting, and then forgot all about me. The sad part was, most of the people in my life treated me that way, and starting today, I was done. I was a strong, smart, independent twenty-five-year-old woman.

We had to stand for the national anthem, so conversation died and then the game started. I was on my feet immediately, cheering and whistling. Though I'd grown up in South Florida, we still considered ourselves New Yorkers. I'd been ten when we moved here from Long Island, so I remembered Mario and another one of my brothers, Roberto, playing hockey when we were growing up.

There were six of us kids, all two years apart. I was the only girl and the youngest, which was another reason I was annoyed. Older brothers were supposed to look out for their little sister, not treat her like an afterthought. Especially after we'd lost our father two years ago to cancer. Mario was the oldest at thirty-five, and twice divorced with no kids. Then came Roberto who was thirty-three and married but no kids yet. Anthony, who went by Tony, was thirty-one and had been with Desi since high school. They'd gotten married right after graduation and had three kids. Salvatore was twenty-nine and engaged, and Peter was twenty-seven and as single as ever.

Then there was me. Twenty-five and struggling to figure out what I wanted to be when I grew up. The only thing I knew for sure was that I didn't want to work in our family pizzeria for the rest of my life. I had big changes coming up that I hadn't told anyone about because I was so tired of being questioned about everything I did, but we had a big family dinner this coming Sunday and I was going to tell everyone about the new developments in my life then.

For now, I lost myself in the game.

This new team, the Lauderdale Knights, had a lot of talent and I'd been the one to propose we buy season tickets for the family. Everyone had hemmed and hawed but finally decided to go in on them with me. The boys all loved hockey too, but I was the biggest fan, so they were happy to alternate going to a game now and then. I planned to be at every damn one. Even if I was late sometimes.

During the first intermission, Desi and I escaped to the ladies' room and she met my eyes in the mirror as we washed our hands.

"You okay?" she asked, cocking her head. "Something's off with you tonight. I know you're mad at the boys, but they can't help it. They're just oblivious sometimes. You've been picking up the slack at the restaurant since your dad died, so they don't give it a second thought."

"They don't give me a second thought," I murmured.

"Old-fashioned Italian boys," Desi said, shrugging. "It's how they were raised."

"That doesn't make it right."

"I feel like there's something else going on," she said, leaning against the counter as I reapplied some lipstick. "Can't you talk to me?"

"I love you," I said gently. "But all you see is the guy you've been in love with your whole life. It's different for me."

"Tony isn't perfect," Desi said, nodding, "but he's a good man. And he loves you. He'll listen if you talk to him. If something is going on at the restaurant and—"

"I've been saying I don't want to work at the pizzeria literally since I was fourteen, and yet, here I am. They wouldn't let me go to college because they said they needed me." I tossed my purse over my shoulder and headed for the exit. "Look, none of this is your fault and I don't want to fight with you about it. Let's just enjoy the game. I'm going to talk to everyone on Sunday about some shit that's bothering me."

She hurried after me. "Your mom has been planning this dinner for weeks—you're not going to do something to ruin it, are you?"

I opened my mouth but closed it again.

This was so typical of my family. I'd just explained how unhappy I was and all she cared about was my mother's dinner party.

This was why I had to get away from the business, and the family to a lesser degree.

Hopefully, sooner rather than later.

***

The Knights were playing the Las Vegas Sidewinders, who'd won the championship last year, so the guys from Lauderdale had something to prove and you could see it. They were playing hard, fighting to win every faceoff, and practically flying up and down the ice. Maybe it was because I was so excited to have a hometown team, or maybe it was the game itself, but I was on my feet for most of it, cheering for the Knights and chirping at the Sidewinders.

When a player named Vaughn Elliott scored the first goal of the game, the season, and the franchise, I was yelling like a lunatic. The whole arena seemed to be on their feet, a sea of orange and blue jerseys, and I forgot all about my personal life, my professional life, and even my annoying family. Hockey was something I'd always loved and since my mother had thought playing hockey wouldn't be ladylike, I'd become a super fan instead.

"Way to put one on the board!" I yelled, clapping as Elliott skated along the bench, high fiving his teammates.

There was one minute left in the second period and most of the crowd stayed on their feet as the Knights won the next faceoff. A defenseman named Zakk Marcus-Cloutier took the puck down the ice and passed it to Elliott. They went back and forth a few times, skating in and around the Sidewinders. Elliott skated up the middle, close to where our seats were, and wound up, taking a slap shot that sent the puck flying.

It went high, up over the glass and in our general direction. Between the lights and everyone around me standing up, I lost sight of the puck. I heard my brother yell my name and I turned just as pain exploded through my head.

Get Slap Shot here!

ALSO BY KAT MIZERA

Las Vegas Sidewinders:

Dominic

Cody's Christmas Surprise

Drake

Karl

Anatoli

Zakk

Toli & Tessa

Brock

Vladimir

Royce

Nate

Sidewinders: Ever After

Jared

Dmitri's Christmas Angel

Ian

Dax (*A Royal Protectors/Sidewinders crossover novel*)

Suze's Diary (A Sidewinders Companion Novella)

Sidewinders: Generations:

Zaan

Tore

Anton

Van

Decker

Alaska Blizzard:

Defending Dani

Holding Hailey

Winning Whitney

Losing Laurel

Saving Sara

Chasing Charli

A Very Blizzard Christmas

Tending Tara

Calling Cassie

Playing Peyton

Catching Lana (An Alaska Blizzard Companion Novel)

St. Louis Mavericks (with Brenda Rothert)

Hard Fall

Hard Limit

Hard Pass

Hard Luck

Hard Hit

Lauderdale Knights:

Knight Before Christmas (A Garland Grove/Lauderdale Knights holiday novel)

Slap Shot

Big Shot

Long Shot

Hot Shot

Sure Shot

Rough Shot

Cheap Shot

Rock Hard:

Play

Pause

Rewind

Fast Forward

Rock Harder:

Rock Bottom

Rock God

ABOUT THE AUTHOR

USA Today Bestselling author Kat Mizera was born in Miami Beach with a healthy dose of wanderlust. She's lived from coast to coast, and everywhere in between, but home is wherever her family is.

A devoted mom and wife to her wonderful and supportive husband (Kevin) and two amazing boys (Nick and Max), Kat loves to travel the globe with her adventurous, hockey loving family. Greece is at the top of that list. She hopes to one day retire there, spending her days writing books on the beach.

Kat is former freelance sports writer who now writes steamy hockey romance about her favorite fictional teams, the Las Vegas Sidewinders and the Alaska Blizzard. The library of novels she's penned also include sexy contemporary stories about baseball stars, alpha sex club owners, special forces heroes, rock stars and royalty. Regardless of genre, her books about bad boys with hearts of gold will steal your breath, rock your world and melt your heart.

WHERE TO FOLLOW KAT:

WEBSITE
FACEBOOK
TWITTER
INSTAGRAM
BOOKBUB
KAT'S PRIVATE FACEBOOK GROUP